THE POET

THE POET

Stephanie Jo Harris

Columbus, Ohio

This book is a work of fiction. The names, characters and events in this book are the products of the author's imagination or are used fictitiously. Any similarity to real persons living or dead is coincidental and not intended by the author.

The Poet

Published by Gatekeeper Press
2167 Stringtown Rd, Suite 109
Columbus, OH 43123-2989
www.GatekeeperPress.com

ISBN (paperback): 9781642373851
eISBN: 9781642373844

Printed in the United States of America

Contents

Chapter 1

"I THINK WE HAVE a small problem. He's being transferred," Nicky said as he came in and shut the door. He stood in the center of a large room, facing an oak desk. Seated at the desk was Vincent Mallo. His office had no windows. Mallo did not care for windows. Instead, his walls were lined floor to ceiling with dark wooden bookshelves. Each book had been cautiously selected by Mallo and placed carefully on the shelf, never to be touched again.

He was a short, thick man with strong Italian features and a smear of black hair that populated only the back and sides of his head. Mallo was, in his own right, slightly connected to *la famiglia in Italia*. He had been placed in New York to assist as needed with other duties as assigned. That is, various backroom dealings, maintaining order with law enforcement, and occasionally converting any idealists that might attempt to fight the good fight. He kept things moving at their regular pace. He was not a brilliant man, but he was smart enough to know a problem when one presented.

"When?" Mallo asked.

"Next week," Nicky replied as he scanned the bookcase, looking for something. Once he selected a book, he stood in front of the desk until Mallo gestured for him to sit.

"Wasn't he part of that thing with Alex?" Vincent asked. Alex had once been seated in the same chair Nicky was in. He and Mallo had a bit of a falling out a few years ago that resulted in, well, some unpleasantness for the man.

"Yeah. He was there for that," Nicky said.

"Transfer. What does that mean to you?" Vincent asked as he poured another glass of brandy.

"It means he's been talking," Nicky said.

"Why was he arrested again?"

"Ag assault. He got into it with somebody at a bar. Drunk, of course. You know how he is. Had some coke on him too."

"He wouldn't turn on ag assault."

"With his record? He would. He's going away for a long time."

Vincent sipped his brandy and thought this over carefully. "Yeah," he agreed.

"Buco won't like it," Nicky added.

"Buco doesn't need to know." Mallo took a sip and added, "Find someone to take care of that."

Nicky did not respond, but he tossed a book of poetry on the desk in front of Vincent. Nicky raised his eyebrows, waiting for an answer. Vincent looked at the book for a few seconds and winced.

"It won't be easy. And it won't be cheap," Nicky finally said.

"Yes," Vincent signed off, still looking at the book.

"I'll take care of it," Nicky said as he rose and left the office.

Chapter 2

"I'M GOING TO kill you!"

Hearing a loud crash from the dayroom, Rebecca set down her coffee in the nurse's station and instructed the staff to call for help. She headed toward the screaming she now heard and saw two of her staff rolling around on the floor, attempting to restrain an agitated patient. When she approached, she calmly asked who was in charge of this episode. The two counselors seemed to relax a bit, regaining composure, and discussed the plan as the rest of the responders arrived. As they moved to help the patient, he began swinging and kicking wildly, so she helped hold one of his legs. He kept fighting, so he was placed in restraints, screaming vulgarities and psychotic statements. He was threatening to kill everyone, to kill her, to kill her staff. They remained professional. She attended the debriefing and thanked everyone for their help as she retrieved her coffee and continued the task of looking in on her units.

When she arrived at her office, she found a pale and

slightly tearful counselor outside her door. "Rebecca, can I have a minute?" the counselor asked.

"Good morning. Of course," she replied with an encouraging smile as they entered her office. "Please sit," she said as she gestured toward a chair and closed the door, all the while trying to remember this person's name. *What was it again? It was unusual. Oh! Esperru! That's right.* She took her seat behind her desk. There was very little visible on Rebecca's desk, only a few papers relevant to the day and her computer. The chaos was well hidden in drawers and filing cabinets.

"How can I help you, Esperru?" Rebecca invited.

"I just . . ." Esperru said as she started to cry. Rebecca grabbed a box of tissues and moved from her desk to the chair next to Esperru, offering her one. Esperru was a newer member of the team, fresh out of school. She seemed so young to Rebecca as she was sitting there, wiping her eyes and struggling to speak. Rebecca waited in silence until the counselor continued.

"I don't know," Esperru finally said. "That was awful."

"Were you hurt?"

She shook her head.

"Was that your first restraint episode?"

She nodded.

"Sometimes those can be frightening," Rebecca said. "I understand. It was very well managed."

"I don't think I can do this."

Rebecca stayed silent, debating the proper route to take. Supportive but honest. It might be true. Not everyone was cut out for this.

"Well," Rebecca said, "I cannot answer that; only

you can. I don't know if you will find this interesting or rewarding. I do, but many people will not. It is unfortunate you cannot tell until you are in the middle of it. This will be unpredictable, and there will be moments you find uncomfortable: times where you question what you experience, and times where you may be afraid. It is all part of this world. If you do find that this is not for you, that is okay. You also may find that you come to love it. I know you have only just started; I recommend you give it a little while before you decide."

Esperru seemed to settle a bit and glanced up at her. Rebecca suspected she had an expectation of being relieved for the day after this trauma.

"In the meantime, I need you back on the unit," Rebecca added. "All right? Talk to your colleagues. They have been there too. You may find that helpful. Stop by the bathroom on your way. Your mascara ran."

Esperru nodded, stood, and hovered at the door. "Thank you," she said softly.

Rebecca nodded, and Esperru returned to the unit. A few minutes later, there was a knock at the door and in walked one of the physicians, loudly complaining about an incident that occurred the prior evening.

"What the hell is going on here? You need to get this place under control!"

"What happened?" Rebecca asked.

He relayed his opinion, angrily and repeatedly. As he spoke, she determined there was no real safety issue here; he was angry someone had questioned him. She listened and placated him with just the right tone, assuring him they would absolutely investigate his concerns and speak with the staff involved. He seemed to be momentarily calm and departed. Just another morning.

Coffee now empty, she prepared for the remainder of the day. After today, she would be on a well-deserved vacation for the next two weeks. At five o'clock, she bolted out the door.

When she returned home, Tom was already there, waiting. She threw on some jeans and made dinner. As they ate, Tom continued to scan his phone and respond to emails.

"How was your day?" she asked.

"Irritating," he said, and then he nodded. "Quite irritating today, actually."

"Why? What happened?"

And so began the drone she had become accustomed to of late. He complained about the challenges of his day, an argument he had with a coworker, the loss of a file he had been working on, the drive home. It was right then that he threw out what she had suspected since the beginning of his tedious rant.

"I don't know about this week. I think I need to stick close to home."

"Oh?"

"Well, unless I do some work from there."

"You can't," she said. "No service."

"What, really?"

"Doesn't everyone know you're off next week?" *You unbelievable jerk.*

"Why do you want to go out there anyway? What are we going to do?" he asked.

"I thought it would be nice."

"Well it's pretty, but still. Why don't we just stay around here?"

She did not respond, but instead cleared the table and turned her focus to scraping plates into the garbage. He did not wait for her to say anything, but instead scanned his phone and retreated to the couch. When she rose to pack he did not stir.

"Are you still going?" With just a hint of surprise in his voice.

"Yes."

"By yourself?" He hesitated and then added, "That's a long drive by yourself."

"It's seven hours; I'll be fine."

"Yeah, but, I mean, you're going alone?"

"It'll be nice to get away. I need a break. I am leaving pretty early, so you probably should go," she said as calmly as possible.

"I can't believe you're acting this way," he said. "You're kind of acting like a child about it. There will be other vacations, Rebecca. Ones we can take together."

"I know. I just want to go, and I already paid for it," she said simply.

"I don't want you going alone."

"I'll be fine, Tom." *I don't remember asking your permission.*

"Fine," he said. "Well, I guess I'll see you when you get back."

"I guess," she agreed.

That night she lay in bed alone, empty, sad, and completely unwanted.

And so she left her little Chicago suburb for her trip.

Vacation alone. Apparently that was now the plan. She had taken the announcement well—at least externally. She was pleased at her ability to avoid the fight he was seeking. She just said she would call when she returned home. There were no phones at this cabin, and she was absolutely not bringing her cell phone with her. It wouldn't matter anyway; there was reportedly no cell service at the resort. Unplugged was the goal, and she intended to remain on vacation for these nine days at this secluded site. After the long drive, she was pleased to find it as quaint and peaceful as advertised.

This place was truly in the middle of nowhere. There were only thirteen cabins, surrounding a lobby restaurant. Cabins 1–6 were on one side of the lobby, and cabins 7–13 were on the other. Each little cabin was entirely rustic, right down to the wood-burning stove and bearskin rug on the floor. It was cozy, "perfect for lovers," as the brochure claimed. Although each cabin was next to another, they were surrounded by a wooden rail and a small deck with a couple of chairs and a fire pit facing the water. Around the lake a small trail and woods, with a gift shop and boathouse on the far end of the resort.

She had spent the last eight days in this bucolic scene pensively considering her relationship, feelings, and life, only to discover a significant lack of satisfaction. And as she sat on the community deck eating breakfast, she was making an internal commitment that her life was about to change.

Rebecca was done.

She was thirty-four years old, after all; time to figure things out.

She was a pretty girl, tall and slender, with short dark hair and brown eyes. She had never been particularly athletic and only slightly funny. She could be interesting and engaging when she had to be, pretty when it was called for, decisive when necessary, but above all, she was smart. She had risen in the ranks of her organization to as high as she could go. Educated in psychology, she had eventually become the administrator of a large inpatient psychiatric unit and learned to navigate both the physical and political dangers that come with such a position. She was successful, but not satisfied. In many respects, Rebecca learned that leadership was only the position no one else wants.

And then there was Tom. She had somehow become involved with this dullard, and she was not sure how to extract herself from this relationship. She met him through work a couple of years ago. He had boyish good looks, blond hair, blue eyes, and a serious manner that proved extremely effective in the financial workings of the facility. He had done well, and he had expensive taste. He would only consider the best items that money could buy. From his car to his perfectly polished shoes, he was the epitome of a successful businessman. When they met, he had pursued her relentlessly, but she could barely remember that phase of their relationship. It used to be flowers, dinners, long walks in the evening; now he was just around. He was not mean, just inattentive and increasingly tedious, and she repeatedly found herself feeling more like part of his image than his girlfriend—just another accessory that needed minimal attention.

This strained relationship had painfully devolved to

the point where he no longer appeared interested in her, was no longer gentle with her, and no longer touched her. It had been at least a year since he had shown any physical interest, despite her playful attempts. She used to put significant effort into being available for him, being ready: shaving her legs, wearing her prettiest undergarments. She kept taking the pill, even though she had not had sex in over a year. Always as ready as she could be. About three months ago when he came over, she had opened the door wearing a very pretty, pink, lacy number. They ended up watching a movie. He said he was tired. Tired. She suspected "he would have been okay with a blow job" kind of tired. She did not indulge him. She no longer tried. This most recent refusal to come with her on vacation, a vacation they had planned together, mind you, had pretty much sealed the fate of yet another sad and unfulfilling relationship.

For Rebecca, being repeatedly physically rejected as a female was not normal, and as such, it was severely damaging and exceedingly painful. So much effort was spent in teaching Rebecca to reject male advances that she never really learned how to endure the same. The longer she was exposed to this environment, the more difficult it became to escape. Once her feelings of worthlessness overcame her confidence, the possibility of rejection became the reality for her. Over these many months of subtle mistreatment, she now found herself riddled with self-doubt and self-loathing. The idea of another man finding her desirable was now an impossibility in her mind. At times, she would look at herself in the mirror, honestly trying to see what was wrong with her. At work, she was in complete control: steady, calm, and decisive. Outside of work was a different story. She felt neither loved nor wanted, neither smart nor attractive. She had recently considered that she might be clinically depressed. She had decided to do her best to look as good as possible here on vacation and to try and push past these feelings of low self-worth. This morning, she had put on a long summer dress patterned with pink and white flowers and her sexiest strappy sandals. She did her hair and makeup, and began the day feeling feminine and pretty. Not that she was exactly looking for some male attention, but she was officially open to the idea.

A group laughed at the table by the end, distracting her from her self-evaluation, and she glanced over. Standing by the entrance to the deck was a pleasant-looking family who appeared to be parting ways. A woman and a younger boy—about twelve, she guessed—were saying their farewells to a rather cute girl, who was probably about fifteen, and an older man. The girl was still wearing her pajamas and had her blond hair thrown up on top of her head. She was slim and pretty, and despite her casual attire and hair, her face was painted perfectly. She and the older man appeared to be staying a few more days. As they returned to the deck and sat down to eat, she scanned the remaining others seated for breakfast.

There was a group of men who sat, unshaven, unsmiling, and not speaking but eating. Here to fish, most likely. There were six of them. All appeared to be around her age, but there was a severity around that table that was palpable. It was as if there had been a terrible fight among them the night before and each man was still angry. A different older couple sat drinking coffee. They appeared weary but happy and seemed ready to depart. *They must be leaving too*, Rebecca thought. Another man sat in the back by himself, wearing a flannel shirt and jeans. He was reading and drinking coffee. He was a big man, and she took from his rugged appearance that he must be a hunter. It was the slow tourist season, and she figured there was only a handful of people still there, to hunt and to fish. She had purposely picked this time of year, the end of August, as the perfect time to book a secluded getaway with her longtime boyfriend and uninterested other party. She felt incredibly foolish for that, considering he refused to come. She rose and refilled her coffee. As she did, she passed the table of angry fishermen.

"Tonight," one of them growled.

"Tonight?" came the response.

"We will have to figure it out."

The table seemed to stir a bit. So apparently they were having some level of unhappy discussion. She walked back to her table and overheard the older man and young girl in a playful banter.

"We'll see, won't we, Grandpa?" the girl said.

"We don't have to see," he said. "I already know. Been coming here ten years, baby girl, and you ain't never been any good at it."

"Fishing has nothing to do with skill," the girl challenged. "It's luck." Rebecca smiled. Despite her perfectly painted face, the girl appeared quite excited to get out on the lake.

The lake was really closer to a large inlet surrounded

by beautiful trees and a small trail. Rebecca planned to spend the majority of the day seated in the sun, reading and relaxing and considering her future. She started walking out to the tree line and heard someone yelling. A man's voice: "Wait!"

She turned around to see one of the angry fishermen and the man wearing the flannel in discussion. She was also surprised to notice they were less than fifteen feet away from her. The fisherman stood facing her as she turned around. He was a rough-looking man, with a brown, unshaven scruff across his face that was less than groomed. His hair was the same—unkempt, it came down to his collar. He looked like a man who was comfortable in the wilderness. The man in the flannel was holding out a five-dollar bill to the fisherman and had a smile on his face, but not in his eyes. A terrible smile. The fisherman seemed to be highly agitated by this for some reason. Looking closer, she noticed the man in the flannel had a subtle, razor-thin line of a scar moving down the left side of his face. It snaked across his forehead and cheek and disappeared beneath his shirt. He was larger than his counterpart, who was glaring at him but not speaking.

Rebecca stood there watching as they stared at each other for what seemed like forever, and finally, the fisherman snatched the money out of his hand, turned, and headed back to the deck. The man with the scar watched him depart and then left. When he passed her, he did not look at her or even in her direction; just kept walking.

Feeling for some reason exposed and uncomfortable, she decided to head back to her room. That exchange had appeared particularly hostile for whatever reason, and it left her wanting to be behind, or at least close to, locked doors. She retreated to her cabin and decided to read on the back deck.

She read for a few hours, had an uneventful lunch, and returned to her room. She stepped outside her door in her bare feet, walked to the rail on the balcony, and lit a cigarette, looking out at the lake. She saw the five dollar man walking along the trail past her cabin. The sky was dark and cloudy, with just a hint of red dashing across the horizon. It was beautiful here. A clinking noise from her left interrupted her, and she turned to see the man that had the strange interaction earlier that day. The one with the scar. He was no longer wearing the flannel, but had on black pants and a dark jacket. She glanced at him in order to socially greet him, but he did not return her gaze. He was staring out over the same lake, glass of wine in his hand. She was irritated at this disruption. Honestly, you don't drive hundreds of miles away from home to an isolated cabin to have someone sitting right next to you. She debated returning to her room, but decided to wait him out. At least until she was done smoking. She returned to looking at the water and heard his door close. She sighed in relief to be alone again—but was also a bit wary. He seemed off. Suddenly, his door opened again, and he held in his hand another wine glass.

"How's the universe today?"

"What?" She turned to face him and said, "I'm sorry?"

"Drink?" he offered, standing next to the rail on his side of the deck, holding out the glass toward her. Rebecca thought perhaps she had misjudged him when she saw him smile. It was a nice smile. She paused before returning a more guarded one and taking the glass.

"Ah, thanks. Cigarette?" She held up the pack. He pulled one out of his jacket and set it on the table. Always nicer to smoke with someone else who was smoking. Much more comfortable. "Did you say something about the universe?"

"I asked you how it was."

She smiled and looked out over the lake. "Seems okay."

"Well, let me know if that changes."

"All right."

He poured her drink and slid his chair closer to her side, the rail separating their cabins between them. She sat back, putting her feet up on the rail in front of her.

"Jack Shelley."

"Rebecca Paige. Pretty here, isn't it?" she offered.

"Very." He was looking at her. "And what do you do, Rebecca?"

"I'm the administrator of a psychiatric facility," she said.

He paused thoughtfully, taking a sip of wine. "A psychiatric facility. I know very little about that." He paused again, thinking. "Is that dangerous?"

"Well, I suppose sometimes. There is a reason there are locks on the doors. Most of the patients aren't a problem; it is mainly the unsick ones that are dangerous."

"The unsick ones?"

"I mean the malingerers, the sociopaths, sometimes the addicts if they are coming down. Really, they all just need help."

"Can they be helped?"

"I believe everyone can be helped," she said simply.

"Do you think they are born that way, the unsick? Or they choose to be that way?"

She was unprepared for depth of this discussion, given she just met this man. She did not have a stock answer for this question and was considering how substantial an answer he really wanted.

"I don't know. Some people think it's biological. Nature versus nurture and all that. I certainly believe in free will, but I think it depends. Some people are probably born with psychological limitations, and the wrong chemicals and environment don't help." Thinking further, she went on, "I have seen some patients who were not able to control their behavior and some who would choose to kill you as soon as look at you. They are all different."

"That sounds unpredictable. Do you like it?"

"Yes," she responded after a moment's thought. "I do."

"Why?" He turned and examined her, appearing genuinely interested.

She took a sip, considering the question and still considering exactly how much she would indulge in this conversation, given he was now asking about more personal matters. Finally, she thought, *Okay, if you really want to know.*

"I like that it's unpredictable. It's challenging; it keeps me steady, keeps me more aware, I think. It's kind of like an adrenalin-fueled mental chess. I can't imagine sitting at a desk all day with the same spreadsheet. When I go to work, I am probably going to hear something I have never heard before, and I like that."

She took a drink. "And what about you? What do you do?"

"I am in risk management."

"And do you like it?" she said with a slight smile, planning on the same line of questioning.

"Are you here on vacation?" he asked. She smiled more, acknowledging his overt and deliberate deflection. She understood his intent for her to be the topic of any and all interrogations.

"Yes. Been here about a week. I leave tomorrow."

"You can't possibly be here alone," he said rather bluntly.

It took her a second to realize the forwardness of the compliment he threw out. She felt herself blush. Rather than answer, she said thank you.

"How is it that you are here alone?"

"Someone cancelled on me. I chose to come anyway." Despite herself, some harshness crept into her voice. He let it pass unmentioned.

"Alone is better," he offered.

"True," she said. "I actually have enjoyed being here by myself. I needed a break."

"I imagine your job carries with it a lot of stress. Probably the type of stress most people don't understand."

"Maybe," she allowed. This man made no attempt at tedious small talk, and she detested small talk.

"Or maybe you needed a break from your absent vacation partner? Or maybe both?" he added.

"Both."

"Both. I see."

"Why are you here alone?" she asked

"I have a work obligation tonight." He thought for a minute. "Also, there's not really anyone I would bring, but you would not have that problem." He glanced at her. "You seem normal. So maybe something happened. A death in the family? Work? Lots of things can lead to sudden cancellations."

"Nope."

"He must be a fool," Jack said simply.

"How do you know it's a he?" she challenged.

"It's a he." he countered, taking another sip of wine. "I don't see a ring. I don't know much about relationships, but I imagine not attending vacation can't be well received."

"It's not."

"Well, maybe you will come home to flowers," he offered.

"Maybe," she said with sarcasm, enjoying this banter. He did not seem to be flirting with her. He seemed to be playfully investigating a new game. She was okay with that right now.

"Too late for flowers then," he said, reading her tone. "Well, it's probably best. Better than being stuck with a fool."

She smiled with the understanding he was just being nice. "Sweet of you. Are you are here for work? Is it a conference or something?"

"No, just an appointment. No conferences with my job. Do you have many conferences you have to attend for work?"

"I am well aware you are changing the subject back to me," she said, smiling.

"How do you feel about that?"

She laughed, fully laughed, at that response, and slightly raised her glass toward him. He smiled back at her.

She had another glass of wine, and he had another cigarette, tossing his empty pack on the table. As the evening wore on, she kept chatting, and she was getting a little light-headed. With her feet perched on the rail, she could feel her sundress licking at her legs in the breeze. Her toes were painted, which pleased her. She was feeling very feminine and, dare say, a bit flirtatious. She was starting to notice how attractive he was. Funny, she didn't notice that before. His eyes were an intense icy blue, and he had dark brown hair that was not styled, but thick and a bit blue collar. He had a nice confidence about him and was actually movie-star good-looking, even with that scar. He was, in a word, intriguing. This was an intelligent and comfortable conversation. He did not seem the slightest bit interested in anything other than just talking to her. The freedom of strangers on vacation. They talked for a couple hours until the last hint of sunlight spread across the lake. Nothing trivial. This man did not seem to do trivial. They talked more about free will and determinism, the nature of evil, the existence of God. By the time the soft lights around the lake were turning on, Rebecca was enthralled.

As they sat looking out toward the water, they could see five dollar man walking down by the pier. He glanced over at them, and Jack gave him the same terrible smile she had seen earlier. The five dollar man looked away.

"Do you know him?"

"No."

"What was that earlier today? Seemed tense."

He finished the last of his wine. "I told him he dropped five dollars."

She was playing the scene over in her head, trying to determine what she may have missed. No one gets that angry over something like that. It didn't make any sense. She held her now empty glass out toward him, and he poured her some more wine. She could feel the questions bubbling up, wanting to ask, knowing there was more. She considered his statement.

"You told him he dropped five dollars," she repeated. "Hmm . . . meaning that maybe he didn't drop anything? That you just said that?"

The very corner of his mouth turned up, but he did not look at her.

"So, what then?" she inquired playfully. "Why would anyone say that if it weren't true? And why would anyone be angry about that?"

"I interrupted him."

"Interrupted him?"

"I thought he might have bad intentions," he said.

She allowed silence, thinking this over, debating again if she should continue this or let it go. "Bad intentions?" she repeated. "You mean related to me?"

He said nothing. Silence fell between them again as she processed this information. She was at once uneasy at this idea and the reality that she did not notice that this person was following her, maybe. She felt very vulnerable.

"He appeared interested in where you were going."

"He did? I guess I am not as aware as I'd like to think,"

she said finally. "So, you did that to let him know you were watching him? That you saw him?" For some reason she was now whispering.

"Not him. I did that to alert you."

"Because I didn't see him." She was angry at herself. "I can't believe I didn't notice."

He glanced at her again. "Maybe you didn't notice him at first, but I think he misjudged you. You would have been the fight of his life."

"That is so . . . um . . . thank you," she quietly stammered a few things, not quite sure if he was teasing her. She was severely impressed by the cleverness of that tactic. That interruption was so simple and unaggressive. The fact that he noticed and intervened on her behalf, maybe, in a manner that was so subtle was rapidly moving him from intriguing to desirable in her mind. She was unsettled, playing over his words, wanting to know more—debating if she really did want to know more. Rebecca suddenly decided to ask him, because this moment, this conversation, would not happen again. "Um . . . why would you say that?"

"I might be wrong." He shrugged. "Could have just been taking a walk and looking at a pretty girl."

"No, I mean about me. Why would you say that?"

"You disagree?"

"Well, in this supposed scenario I'd like to think so, but how other people see us is not usually how we see ourselves."

"It is never how we see ourselves."

"You are not answering the question." She smirked at him.

"You're right." He smiled. "People do not usually catch me doing that."

"Well?"

"Confidence," he said finally. "You project confidence, intelligence, warmth, and caution. It is an interesting blend. How do you see yourself?"

Rebecca looked down and felt herself blush. What he had described was not how she saw herself, but rather everything she wanted to be. He was looking at her, watching her, waiting for a response. All she could do was shrug.

"How do you see me?" he offered, politely removing her from her current state.

"Well, situationally, at first I assumed you were a hunter."

"A hunter."

"At breakfast. I thought you were a hunter."

"That is an activity. You are not answering the question either."

"That's true." She laughed. "I guess at first I thought you were a bit intimidating. Maybe? No offense."

"How honest of you," he remarked. "Would you like to take a walk with me around the lake to the gift shop?"

"Yes," she said simply. "I need my shoes." She slowly walked into her room. Once inside, she quickly debated between the sexy sandals or practical tennis shoes. She decided on sexy sandals. She visited the restroom and glanced at herself in the mirror, quickly fluffing her hair. For some reason, she felt as if she needed to rush. As if this small interruption might alter the playful banter and intelligent conversation she had somehow managed to find in this wilderness. Was she just debating the nature of evil with a tall, dark stranger?

That was arguably one of the best conversations I have ever had. I can't remember the last time I discussed such things, such glorious things. Not the lake, not the type of wine preferred or the annoying reasons surrounding the best route to take on this drive to the cabin, not the weather or any of the other endless items strangers discuss. He asked me about my thoughts on free will and debated me on the issue. What was his opinion there? He never said. I have to watch that. He is an expert at not answering questions. I really like this man.

She stopped at the mirror.

Confident, intelligent, warm, and cautious; I might sleep with this man.

No, Rebecca. You won't. You don't even know him. You know you don't do that.

You would be the fight of his life. You can't possibly be here alone.

Still . . . I think I might.

"Calm down, Rebecca," she mumbled.

When she came back out, he was waiting next to her door. She felt pleasantly adolescent as they walked down the deck. The night was warm but not humid, and a very slight breeze came across the lake. She kept her hand at her side, open and ready should he feel the urge to take it. He didn't.

"Tell me about this fool. What does he do?" He matched her pace as she walked.

"His name is Tom." She was starting to think maybe he was interested in something other than conversation.

That was good, since she had already decided *yes* when she was picking out her shoes. "I don't know. He's thirty-five, finance officer, professional, friendly, smart. We've been together a couple of years. It's more like a habit now."

"Smart," he repeated. "Would people say he's good-looking? Wealthy?"

"Yes, probably."

"I see. What else? Tell me what he doesn't do."

"What he doesn't do. Well let's see . . ." She was just tipsy enough to have this conversation. "He doesn't come on vacation with me," she said playfully. "He doesn't really talk to me anymore. He doesn't seem to listen. He doesn't touch me." She trailed off a bit; that last one hurt to actually say out loud. Jack gave no visible response. "What about you?" Realizing she had taken an accidental serious turn, she tried to change the subject. "You must have some young, hot female running around your apartment in her underwear?"

"Why would you say young and hot?"

"Well, let's see. What are you? Thirty-five?"

"Thirty-seven."

"Okay," she smiled. "I say young because you seem the type to prefer more casual acquaintances, and they would find you an intriguing older man, grounded and a little scary. I say hot because you're good-looking, quiet, and confident. You certainly know how to get women to open up; you have been reflecting everything I've said for the past few hours." She nodded, pleased with her assessment. "I would bet they follow you around."

He smiled. For the briefest of moments, she thought

she saw desire in his eyes. They entered the gift shop. When he went to retrieve whatever it was he needed, she stepped into the ladies room. Again, she needed solitude and a glance in the mirror. Standing there, she started to take stock of this situation. Her breathing was faster than normal; she tried to calm down, holding onto the sink. She looked deeply into the mirror, and with a fluff of her hair and a final deep breath, she exited the bathroom, and they walked out of the shop. They had stopped speaking, and for Rebecca, there seemed to be a new intensity to this little journey. As they stepped onto the trail leading back to the cabins, he moved from her right side to her left. She suspected maybe this was due to his scar.

"You stopped speaking," he said.

"Oh no, it's not . . . I just know I have been doing all of the talking. I'm getting tipsy," she stammered. "Why don't we talk about you?"

"All right."

From behind them, the elderly couple she had noticed at breakfast was entering the gift shop. The woman was speaking in another language; it sounded Italian. She touched her husband on the arm and gestured toward them. She noticed Jack smile.

"You speak Italian?" she asked.

"I know a few phrases."

"What? Were they talking about us?"

"You. She said, 'Isn't she beautiful?'"

"She did?" Rebecca smiled and glanced behind her to see the elderly couple who had moved inside. She could no longer see them, so she turned back to keep walking on the trail.

And then she fell.

Perhaps it was the two glasses of wine she had, the uneven terrain, or the sexy sandals, but she stumbled. As she fell, her hand reached out blindly to steady herself. It landed directly against the side of his chest, feeling the hard steel underneath his jacket. She recoiled as if she were burned and pulled back, looking at him. He grabbed her elbow and was still wearing the hint of a smile when he asked her if she was okay. The smile was gone in an instant at the look in her eyes.

He knew she knew.

He kept his hand firmly on her elbow.

They stood. Her mind was racing, yelling out various commands to run, pretend she hadn't noticed, scream, yell at him—all not very good options. It dawned on her that she had managed to end up one hundred miles from anywhere, alone in the dark with a man with a gun. A dangerous man. That explained his intensity. A silent and cold indifference hung around him, and it seemed so obvious she did not know how she had missed it before. It started to sprinkle rain very lightly, tickling her neck with the breeze caressing her skin.

"All right," he said decidedly. Holding her arm, he walked her off of the path and into the dark behind the small boathouse along the dock. He did not pull her toward him, but stepped into where she was until she felt her back was against the wooden frame. Still holding her elbow, he kept moving closer until he was only inches away, and he placed his other hand on her throat. He towered over her. She could hear her breath coming fast, heart racing, and she was starting to shake.

He leaned in and looked deeply into her frightened eyes. His face was different now. The comfort that she thought had surrounded him, if it had ever been there in the first place, was gone. What she saw now was momentarily terrifying. There was no anger, just cold; inhuman. His eyes reflected a detached sort of look as he tilted his head slightly to the side, examining her briefly.

"Jack?" Rebecca whispered.

"Shh. Be still," he ordered quietly. She did not move. He lowered his head, very gently resting his forehead against hers. He stayed there and breathed her in.

She could hear her pulse in her ears. As her mind whirled around the possible endings to this scenario, she was interrupted by his intensity, his breath against her skin. His intimate closeness and the feel of his forehead resting lightly against hers. His hand softly placed around her throat no longer felt frightening. It felt more as the hand of a lover, tender and inviting. That's not to say she did not feel fear, but beyond fear, what she felt was akin to disappointment. Rebecca recognized that, even now, she was only slightly afraid of him; but she was intensely attracted to him. His forehead moved to the side until his cheek rested against hers. His mouth at her ear, hand on her throat. It was warm against her skin, and she could feel the pulse in her neck pushing against his palm.

It seemed like hours before he finally spoke.

"Are you afraid of me?"

"Yes."

"You *are* beautiful," he whispered. A soft whimper escaped her. She was still frozen against the wall. His hand moved from her neck, slowly and firmly across to her shoulder, and down her arm. He stayed there a few seconds longer and then stepped back, again holding her elbow. She looked at him weakly.

He let out a breath, long and slow.

"I will walk you back," he said in a way that was not a suggestion. He let go of her arm. Rebecca decided running would be futile. He would snatch her up like she was a child. Also, she did not think she could trust her legs. They walked back to the room in silence. She stood there with her heart racing, damp hair clinging to the sides of her cheeks. She was trying to slow her breathing.

"Are you a cop?" she asked in a quiet voice.

"No." His response was steady and unapologetic.

She tried not to look at him, tried to hide the obvious fear and desire that was there. The rain had picked up a bit, steady now as they stood under the roof next to her door. Thunder spread across the night. When she reached for her key, it dropped to the ground. He knelt immediately at her feet to find it, and with that movement, she felt safe with him. She knew he was dangerous; but she also knew that he was no danger to her. Watching him drop to his knees, as a gentleman would, his face was calm, his movement relaxed; he had no plan to hurt her. That now established, she thought again of him moving her into the dark and saying she was beautiful. Not bad, that. Very raw. This man seemed so powerful and so commanding . . . so dangerous.

What would it be like, to be with him? Come, dangerous man. Come say dark and beautiful things to me.

She decided she didn't care. She didn't care about the gun. She wanted to be held, wanted to feel beautiful again, wanted to feel desired. She wanted this man. As he knelt at her feet to collect her key, she impulsively tilted her knee up next to his cheek. Jack leapt to attention. He paused for only a moment before he stepped in and kissed her. She slid her hands into his hair while he opened the door and backed her into the room.

Her room was dark, lit only by the moon through the window. Jack kissed her mouth, her cheek, her neck, sliding his hands into her hair, across her shoulders, her hips. He kissed her fearlessly, and she started to tremble. Rebecca settled into him. Her hands moved to his chest and under his coat. Suddenly, he grabbed her wrists and pushed her roughly against the wall. Rebecca cried out, eyes wide with surprise.

Jack released her wrists and stepped back. He took his gun from beneath his coat, glanced around, and placed it on the nightstand. When he turned back toward her, Rebecca was already gripping the doorknob, a second away from bolting from the room. He noticed her hand and stopped his approach, but he did not offer any apology. This was not safe, and he made no effort to make it appear that way. Instead, he looked like a ravenous predator that would devour her.

She realized her hand was on the doorknob and withdrew it. She took a step closer to him, but he did not move. Rebecca was still shaking, and her wrists were really starting to hurt, but she did not let him see that. *He reacted. He just reacted. He thought I was going for his gun.*

"It's all right," she whispered.

His eyes narrowed in suspicion, and his head tilted very slightly. She placed her hand on his cheek.

"It's all right," she said again, stronger this time.

He softened. He pressed his cheek against her hand, turned in, and kissed her wrist. He picked up the other wrist and did the same, then placed her hands back on his chest. His mouth hovered over hers, giving her a chance to stop him. She didn't. His kiss, gentler this time, deepened again, down to her neck, hands sliding down the sides of her body. He felt so good. Everything about him was so severe. There was no pretense, no hesitation. *This man owns me tonight.*

"How could anyone not touch you?" Jack whispered, mouth against her neck. She whimpered and melted against him. He stopped and picked up his gun. "I have to go," he said. "I will be back in a couple hours. I will knock. Maybe you will let me in."

He left her standing breathless in the center of the room.

If anyone were watching, they would have noticed him pause by her door, hand lingering on the doorknob. He put on his gloves, retrieved a bag from his room, and returned to his car.

He drove east for twenty-five minutes, and reaching the first stoplight, he pulled to the side of the road. He stepped out into the darkness and approached. He pulled out his HK45 with sound suppressor and shot it two times, causing a slew of angry sparks and the light to begin to flicker red. He returned to his car and drove on, approaching the small town that was about one-half hour east of the cabin resorts. He drove farther until he arrived at the second stoplight, where he did the same thing, shooting the stoplight until it too flickered red.

He drove about a block, pulled into a small gas station that was isolated on the corner, and parked along the side of the building as far from the parking lot lights as possible. Here he shut off the car and waited. After a while, he exited the car and, in the rain, turned up his collar and pulled his dark wool cap to his eyebrows. He moved through the shadows to the corner where the closest now-flickering stoplight was, and knelt down next to a row of bushes on the corner. Several minutes later, a large vehicle appeared, but instead of passing the gas station as expected, it turned into the station, coming to rest in front of the entrance. He watched as two officers emerged, one heading into the gas station and the other standing next to the driver's side door. The vehicle was a transport unit. The guards did not concern him. His interest was on the inside.

He remained motionless, evaluating. Once decided, he moved quickly in the darkness, approaching the officer who remained by the vehicle. Stealth on approach, and shielded by the noise from the rain, he was immediately behind the officer, gun pointing at the back of his head.

"On your knees, hands behind your back."

It was evident the officer was taken completely off guard; he hesitated, stammered a protest, and complied. Jack handcuffed the officer to a pole next to the truck and removed his weapon and Taser. He searched him briefly, also removing his keys, phone, and radio, which he tossed into the open door of the vehicle.

"Face down. Stay silent." Again, the officer complied.

He entered the gas station.

Chapter 3

Janice stood behind the counter. She was a heavy woman, sloppy, with long hair that was a darker red than it should have been. This was accented by fierce lipstick that was too bold for her skin. She applied multiple layers of black eyeliner to brown eyes that used to be pretty, but now were tired and slightly bitter. Her hair came past her shoulders in a long, scraggly manner that was once stylish, but now only unflattering. In fact, all the attention she had given to her looks ended up making her look older then she really was. Janice was always slightly annoyed, always slightly arrogant. Her friends were not really her friends. She kept them around as a form of mild amusement so she could have someone to manipulate. She leaned heavily against the counter, preening in the mirror next to the register. It was around ten thirty, and she knew she would have no real customers on a night like tonight. She was preening in case Officer Marcus came. He was a cutie, and it was a long night. She smiled as the bell rang over the door. It was really raining outside now, and the man who entered stopped to shake off his coat.

Marcus had been on the force for about fifteen years. He was tall, slightly overweight, and handsome in a delicate sort of way. He was no stranger to getting his hands dirty if the job demanded. He was known as being a hard worker and all-around nice guy, if not slightly dull. For the past few years, he and Kalo had been transporting prisoners from the state facility to whatever new arrangement awaited them. It was decent work and not particularly challenging, as long as you followed the rules. Of late, he had become partial to stopping in to chat with Janice and flirt a bit. She had a way of making a man feel important. She always kept the look of possibility in her eye.

"Officer Marcus!" she purred. "Why, what brings you out here on such an awful night?"

"Hi, Janice. Looking good, girl," he said as he approached the counter. "Got one hell of a character out there." He loved to tease her with the dangers of his job. "Wanted to check in on you before we went on, make sure you're doing all right."

What happened next, according to the witnesses, and what little was available from the surveillance footage, occurred in a matter of seconds. The bell sounded the opening of the door. A man moved quickly and directly toward the counter. Simultaneously, his right hand rose, shooting the camera above the counter, while his left hand shot the Taser, striking Officer Marcus in the leg. Officer Marcus screamed in surprise and collapsed on the floor in a twitching pile. The gun moved from the camera and pointed at Janice's face.

"Don't move."

The man knelt down and rolled over the now subdued officer, cuffing his hands behind his back. Immediately, he crossed behind the counter to the now pale and terrified Janice.

"On your knees. Hands behind your back."

She knelt down, squeaking, "Please don't . . ."

Taking a zip tie from beneath his jacket, he tied her hands securely behind her back and grabbed her arm. He pulled her up to her feet and half walked, half dragged her into the open door behind the register. Placing her there, he returned to Officer Marcus, who was now starting to moan and issue threats of arrest and other such warnings. Without a word, the assassin grabbed him by the collar and slid him across the floor, piling him next to Janice. He searched him briefly, removing his keys, radio, gun, and phone, and tossed them outside of the door. He returned outside to Kalo, wet and struggling on the ground next to the truck. Kalo was starting to get to his feet. The assassin assisted him, cuffed his hands behind his back, and walked him into the back room, tossing him down to the floor. He scanned the room, stepped past Janice, Marcus, and Kalo, and ripped the phone from the wall and threw it next to Officer Marcus's belongings. Shutting off the light, he closed the door. He paused at the counter and took a pack of cigarettes. While walking to the back of the store, he tore open the pack, scanning the walls of the station. As he moved, he took a disposable razor off of the rack and put it in his pocket. Seeing the breaker box, he opened it up and turned off the main breaker, plunging the room into darkness. Outside, he stopped and put a cigarette in his mouth. Arriving at the truck, he opened the back door and stepped inside.

A man was seated toward the front of the cab, handcuffed to a ring in the center of the vehicle. In the light of the cab, his face transformed from joy to terror as he saw what he believed to be his rescuer turn out to be something else entirely. Gun in hand, the assassin moved toward him and placed a cigarette in his mouth. He lit it and stepped back, sitting next to the door.

Silence.

"It's you, huh," the dead man said. "I can't believe it. You gotta know this ain't right. He knows I'm no rat. He *knows* that! Call him and see. Get him on the phone, please—you are making a mistake here. He knows I would never rat on him."

"He doesn't know that," the assassin said.

"Please . . ." the man said, meeker this time, weak and desperate.

"Last requests?"

Silence.

"Peace with God?"

"Why start now?" the man said painfully, sadly, through clenched teeth. He was starting to sweat.

Silence.

"You know . . . . someday it will be you on the other side of this gun," he growled.

"Perhaps."

The cigarette burned to its last. The dead man dropped

it and stepped on it, looking down. He did not raise his head.

Gun leveled, two shots.

The assassin stepped lightly out of the van, closing the door behind him. Keeping his extinguished cigarette in his mouth, he moved to the front of the van and climbed inside. He backed it up next to the gas station in the dark and returned to his car.

Chapter 4

REBECCA SMILED AND flopped down in the empty bed. She felt immediately whole. It was shocking, really, how good she felt, even considering he had departed. Oh well, he had to go to work. No matter; he was coming back. Coming back to finish what he started. She smiled again. Surprising how a brief make out session with a handsome stranger essentially healed two years of painful self-hatred. She honestly could have spent thousands on therapy where some counselor could have tried to explain to her how she was worthy of affection and she really was a good and decent person that men find appealing, but she didn't need it anymore. Granted, she knew she should not need a man's touch to feel good about herself. She also knew that apparently that is exactly what she needed. Noted and accepted. All the anger and pain she had been carrying were gone—just like that. She felt beautiful and sexy and, damn it, like a woman again. And as for feeling any guilt about cheating on her pseudo-relationship . . .

He should have come with me.

She wasn't too surprised. To be honest, Rebecca knew women had their ways. Ignore your woman long enough, and she might have sex with the first man to call her beautiful. Anyone. Pizza man, delivery man, that guy at the gas station that held the door open and smiled at her. Who he was did not matter. If he was eager and slightly attractive, that was helpful. If he was gallant and ruggedly handsome, well, not even her fault, really. For Rebecca, this was not out of spite or rage. It was only about her.

She rose to shower, running her hands across her body, reliving his touch. How perfect it was. How perfect he was. Talking to him, kissing him—how he held her so well. He had not even attempted to remove her clothing. Actually, his hands never strayed beyond a gentleman's touch, effectively making her want him more . . . And he had a gun.

Nope. Not entirely ready to think about that yet, but it was too late. It was there. *He did have a gun, and he did leave earlier to go out and do something with that gun. And now what? Now what indeed? Do I ask about it? How can I not? What exactly is the appropriate relationship protocol when you learn your would-be lover is armed?* She did know one thing, though. When he did knock, she most certainly was going to let him in. In fact, she couldn't wait.

She mostly dried her hair, enough to look good, and pulled on her jeans and black T-shirt. The night was a bit brisk, so she ditched the sexy sandals and retreated to socks and tennis shoes. Slipping on a flannel, she returned to the front deck to watch the storm and wait for him. She still felt like she was in a trance—that wonderful feeling that comes from a passionate kiss. She felt sexy and happy, reliving every touch. She remembered how he had responded to the just the slight tilt of her knee. How he had stepped in and paused before he kissed her. How he had said she was beautiful. She sank back into the chair and slid her legs back up on the rail. She almost writhed in her seat with the intensity of it all, and the soft smile would not leave her mouth. Somehow the horror she had felt when she discovered the gun was entirely gone.

Amazing what you can get used to.

She wasn't quite sure how long she had been sitting there, at least three cigarettes worth of time, when she heard the first scream. It cut through the silence, and she bolted upright in her chair, listening intently in the night.

Silence.

Then a woman's voice screaming, "No! Please don't!"

She leapt from her chair and ran into her room, locking the door behind her. She started searching frantically around the room for her car keys. As she grabbed them, a loud bang sounded, and her door smashed open. There were two men there with guns drawn. She froze.

"Let's go. Lobby," one of them said.

She walked out of the room with them at her heels. She could feel her body starting to shake and her breath quickening. She could also feel her pulse and the rest of the body's normal reaction to fear. She was consciously struggling to keep this in check, to think clearly and not react.

Upon entering the lobby, she briefly paused at the door until she felt a hand at her back, shoving her forward. She walked in, straight ahead, and went to the small table next to the bar. She sat facing the room and started to evaluate. To her right, seated on a large, plush couch, were the grandfather and the young girl. She was there next to him, his arm around her protectively. He was older, but she could feel the rage coming off of him as he sat there like a wild creature guarding its young, even more so as this young was female and, as such, more likely subject to specific punishments of horror and severity. She was a pitiful thing. She had her knees drawn up to her chest, and frightened tears rolling down her cheeks. She must have been sleeping when they came, for she was wearing a thin white pair of pajamas that had been soaked in the rain. Her young body was quite visible through the clothes, small but noticeable breasts forcing their way through a flimsy spaghetti string top. Rebecca also noticed Mr. Five Dollar's uncomfortable interest in this young girl. He was now armed and standing at the door, eyes shamelessly roving up and down her body. Without a word and without much thought, Rebecca stood and took off her flannel. She crossed the room as casually as possible and stopped in front of the young girl, handing her the shirt.

"Put this on and stop crying." And then, quieter, she added, "He likes that." Rebecca was regretful to have to tear innocence from this girl and to be the one to put *that* thought in her head, but her time for innocence was now required to be over. *Yes, dear, they are out there. Some men enjoy making you cry. Some men can't get enough of it.* It worked. The girl grabbed the shirt and dove into it as if it were the most precious item of clothing ever received. Rebecca remained in front of her until she had the shirt closed around her. Her tears subsided somewhat. Rebecca did not look at the grandfather and his look of rage and gratitude. She couldn't bear it.

She returned to her place at the bar. The elderly couple was seated to her left. They were silent, holding hands and looking at each other with sadness. The woman was obviously starting to pray, and her endearing husband just held her, softly stroking her leg. Rebecca ripped her eyes from that scene as she feared she might tear up, which was not helpful right now; she saw to the right of the old couple two other gentlemen she had not noticed earlier. Sizing them up, she had the impression they may be here for some sort of flower festival or bird-watching event. They did not appear to be the type of men who hunt. Each was dressed in silky pajamas, slippers, and robes. She did not think they were a couple because of the distance between them. Brothers, maybe. One sat on the end of the couch, and the other in the chair next to him. Each seemed frail, with complacent and silent eyes to the ground, awaiting further instruction. Some sort of scholars perhaps, here to study the migrating finches or whatever. She felt a hard gaze and discovered Mr. Five Dollar was glaring at her for her move with the flannel. She looked away, not wanting to anger him further. It was evident he was not at liberty to prevent her from covering the girl for some reason. There were three of them at the doorway: five dollar, bearded guy, and another one with a shaved head. Shaved head was obviously in charge of this operation. He was maybe around six feet tall, pale, and the most serious of the three. He would have been attractive had he not been so menacing, and he was looking her. He turned to bearded guy and sent him to search the rest of the cabins.

"Go watch the road," he added to unseen individuals standing outside. After a few minutes, Rebecca stood up like she owned the place and moved behind the bar.

"Does anyone want a drink?" she asked, keeping her voice as calm and steady as possible.

Silence.

She removed from the bar a half empty bottle of wine and a wine glass, and took both back to the table with her. She emptied the bottle, placed it on the table within reach, and sat down. *Better than nothing*, she thought. She did indulge in one glorious sip of wine. It was spectacular. Starting to feel panic creeping up on her again, she rose, crossed behind where she had been sitting, opened up the door that led to the screened-in deck and smoking area, and sat back down. A delightfully cool breeze wafted through the room, and the sound of the rain outside was somehow comforting. She lit a cigarette and gazed longingly out the door at the storm—how beautiful, how powerful. A brief sadness hit her with thoughts of life unlived, things undone. Sadness at the loss. She thought of Jack. *These men must be here for him. What else could it be?*

Crying came from the doorway, and in came the woman who owned this place. She had to be about sixty years old—retirement venture, perhaps. She was a sturdy woman; silent tears rolled down her cheeks. She was dressed in a long, well-loved blue nightshirt and old slippers. Her graying hair was free flowing, stopping just short of her shoulders. According to the short biography on the menu, Margaret ("but you better call me Peggy") and her late husband, Marvin, had purchased this resort a few years ago to bring peace and tranquility to people who needed to just "get away." That is what the breakfast menu had said: "Come GetAway with us!" Underneath that caption was a sweet photo of Peggy and Marv seated next to the little gift shop in two rockers, smiling and welcoming to the camera.

The guy with the shaved head joined Peggy at the door and then spoke to them all.

"Do what we say, and no one will get hurt."

He then turned his attention to Peggy and said, "You are going to call your son. You are going to tell him to come here now."

"What?" she said honestly confused. "Please, what do you want?" she asked through tears.

His response was to hand her the only working phone at the resort and point a gun at the elderly couple seated on the couch. His first action was to threaten the most vulnerable of the poor vacationers, not to threaten Peggy herself. Ruthless, highly effective, and not up for negotiation. Peggy screamed, and he slapped her lightly across the face. She was crying, and with a shaking hand, she took the phone and dialed. After a few minutes, she said the voicemail picked up.

"Keep trying. Leave him a message that he needs to come here now."

"Stay here and find me when she reaches him," he instructed five dollar and stepped outside. Five dollar slid a chair over next to the woman and sat down, laying the gun across his lap.

The man with the shaved head reappeared in the lobby. When he approached Rebecca, she looked down obediently. He reached behind the bar and picked up an ashtray, setting it in front of her.

"Do you have what you need?" he asked intently, knowingly. His eyes were close to black, commanding authority and clearly indicating she should not move again.

"Yes," she whispered. He returned to the doorway.

For Rebecca, years of working on a psychiatric unit had taught her many things. Whispers can work better than yelling; giving and receiving respect is highly effective; never, ever trust a patient; always keep one hand open; never let anyone block the exit; everything is a weapon; keep your back to the wall . . . and never let anyone see you are afraid. These acts of opening the door, getting a drink, playing hostess, these were not only acts of respect and social grace; they were acts of testing authority. These were methods to see how severely she was being monitored. How interested were her captors in her behavior? Even from outside, the man with the shaved head was interested. How interested were her companions? Well, not interested at all.

She kept looking around the room, eyeing each of the other guests. She was searching for someone or something that might prove useful. Anything. Because she was completely aware that she would probably die tonight, it was just a question of how.

Chapter 5

THE ROADS WERE desperately black. The threatening storm had fully arrived, and the windshield wipers and lights did little to provide visibility for Jack as he drove cautiously in the direction of the cabin. The car passed the first flickering stoplight and continued west, stopping briefly at the second stoplight. Just enough time in between for someone to enter a vehicle at the first light, shoot someone inside, and then exit at the second light, leaving the driver completely unaware. Much preferred to what had happened, but killing cops attracted unrelenting attention. Besides, he was only paid for one.

As the car approached the slight fork in the road with the small wooden sign pointing in the direction of the GetAway Resort, it slowed almost to a stop. Eventually, it moved again, turning left onto the gravel road to GetAway, and the car picked up speed. This torrential rainfall was creating significant areas of standing water on the road, and driving was becoming more difficult. The car began to slide to the left, and slide, and slide, and finally lost all traction to the point of a slow descent off of the road and into the now flooded ravine below. It came to rest squarely in the ravine, and Jack could feel water seeping in up to his ankles. His response was to lay his head against the back of the seat and swear softly.

"Pay you back, Eddie," he growled. Eddie owned a small used car dealership in the neighborhood. Over the years, he and Jack had developed a sort of relationship that allowed Jack, for a small fee, to borrow the occasional vehicle without having to put his name on anything.

He roughly opened the door while more water rushed in, and cautiously exited the car. As he did, he felt the door fighting him. He pushed back and, in the process, sliced his forearm about four inches across. He hissed. Reaching back into the passenger seat, he removed his now soaking bag from the floor and the keys from the ignition. He stood in the rain; unaffected, he unzipped the bag and began to empty the contents into the ravine. He took one T-shirt and wrapped it on his arm; he threw the other shirts and pants into the dark water ahead. Reaching farther in the car, he pulled out a flooded box of bullets, which he emptied, throwing handfuls at a time out into the night. The car itself shifted and floated into deeper water. Finally, he threw the bag and car keys in and began to embark on a more irritating than treacherous ascent back to the road.

No sooner had he set foot on the gravel than the rain subsided to a soft drizzle. He turned up his collar and started walking toward the resort along the side of the road. Upon his approach, he heard someone cough. He froze. Kneeling down slowly, he pulled closer to the tree line, examining the source of the sound.

"How long do we have to stand out here in this shit?"
"Shut up."

Following the voices in the dark, he could barely see two individuals standing along the road, one on the side of the entrance to GetAway and the other in the middle of the street. He could also see the one in the middle was holding a handgun. Uncertain, he drew his weapon and watched this duo, considering. They remained where they stood, and did not speak again.

He turned into the woods and continued his approach to the cabins. He did not hurry. He was comfortable in the hopelessly dark. His movement was easy within the trees, and the rain guarded any noise he might make. He followed the tree line all the way up to where it halted, past the lobby and adjacent to the parking area next to the row of cabins. He stepped out and crouched down next to one of the cars there, peering through the side window. As he scanned the cabins, paying more than a little attention to cabin 12, he could see each door was wide open, with the light from each room spilling out onto the walkway between them. One man appeared to be going from room to room, checking for occupants. Two other men were pushing Rebecca down the walkway and into the lobby. All three of the men were armed. The moon crept out, and the assassin noted the glint from a set of keys dangling from the ignition of the car he was leaning against. He looked at them briefly, set his jaw, and began a slow approach within the shadows toward the cabins.

Chapter 6

"WHAT DO YOU mean, someone is missing?" the man with the shaved head inquired.

"The registry. Someone is missing," Mr. Five Dollar said.

"Who is missing here?" the man with the shaved head demanded of the owner. Shaken, but done crying for now, Peggy slowly reached for the registry, read it, and silently counted off the guests in the lobby.

"Eleven," she finally said. "The guest from cabin 11. He is supposed to be checking out tomorrow. Maybe he left early?"

"Name?"

"Jack Shelley."

Mr. Five Dollar sat up, suddenly interested in this conversation.

"Yeah, that fucking guy. Fucking asshole. I saw him. Where is that guy? I want to talk to him some more."

"Go check 11 and see if there is anything in there: toothbrush, clothing, whatever," came the order, and the bearded guy went about his task.

"She knows him," five dollar offered, gesturing to Rebecca. "They were all cozy earlier."

The man with the shaved head picked up the registry.

"Rebecca Paige? Cabin 12?" Rebecca looked at him with her most innocent and confused face. Boss man crossed the room and sat at the table with her, allowing his presence to settle around her.

"Is he coming back?"

"I don't know," she said quite honestly.

"What do you know?"

"Nothing. I just met him."

Boss man, recognizing this game, stood up, violently grabbing her by the throat. He slammed her against the wall and tightened his grip. Peggy screamed. Rebecca's hands went up instinctually to his arm, pulling feebly against his hand, unable to breathe. He held her there for a few seconds before he released his grip, allowing her air, but keeping his hand firmly around her neck. She started coughing and wheezing, trying to regain herself.

"Tell me what you do know."

"He said his name was Jack. I met him tonight. His cabin is next to mine. We shared a glass of wine and took a walk to the gift shop." She spoke quickly, information only, and fully allowed her voice to tremble. *Yes, boss man, you are in charge, and I will do as you say.*

He stood there holding her throat, looking into her eyes, seeking out the truth. "Are you lying to me?" he said with a sinister tone. She did not respond.

"Tell me about him. What does he look like?"

"White, tall, big, bigger than you—maybe six two, six three? Brown hair, blue eyes, thin scar on his cheek."

His hand tightened on her throat again. "What did you say?" he whispered.

She tried to respond but couldn't speak. Her mouth opened and closed in an attempt, and her hands again went to his arm, pulling against him, trying to breathe.

"Nothing in the room," bearded guy returned with his report. "It is empty. Towels hung up, drawers empty, nothing."

"Go keep watch on his cabin."

Boss man let go of her neck, and Rebecca started gasping in air. He took her arm and walked her back to her seat. After taking a glass from the bar, he poured himself wine and sat next to her.

"You are going to tell me everything you know about this man."

"Okay . . ." she stammered, allowing her eyes to briefly flash to five dollar man seated in the doorway. Boss man followed her gaze and spoke to him.

"Matt?"

"Huh?"

"What do you know about this guy?"

"Nothing. This morning we got into it a bit. Fucking asshole. Told me I dropped some money, that's all," he trailed off. "Nothing—really, David, I just saw his face, that's all."

Turning back to Rebecca, he took a drink and asked, "Are you here alone?"

"Yes."

"Why?"

"Someone cancelled on me." She refused to meet his gaze. She cautiously doubted her ability to lead with this particular dance partner.

"Are you sure you aren't here to meet Mr. Shelley? A romantic getaway, perhaps? Some time away? What is it that you are not telling me?" he said seductively. "If I were to shoot one of these people, would that change what you remember?" As he spoke, he pulled out a gun and laid it on the table, his hand resting on top of it.

"Nothing, I don't know. I think he said he was from Chicago," she offered weakly. "I did not want to know him. We had a conversation; we shared some wine and a cigarette. I said I had to go to the gift shop, and we walked down there together. When we got back to my room, he left. He walked toward the parking lot." With everything in her, she dove into this lie, believed it, lived it, delivering each timid and frightened statement with what she hoped was the perfect amount of fear and innocence. "I was kind of afraid of him." True.

"Tell me about this scar." She was right. They had come here for him.

"It was thin, barely visible. On the left side of his face. I think it went from his forehead, over his eye, and down his cheek to his neck." She was focused on the gun. *They will kill who they kill. I will not tell you. I will not. You are going to kill us anyway.*

"Rebecca, where was he was going?"

"I have no idea. He didn't say."

"Do you think he is coming back?"

"No."

She did not lie out of any perceived affection or obligation to the dark man with whom she had shared such a brief encounter. She did not lie out of some fantastic belief that he may come for her, may save her and the others. She lied because these men were threatening her with guns, and whatever she could do, however inconsequential, she intended to be difficult. She already knew they were going to kill her. It would not matter if she told them he planned to return, and they certainly did not need to know he was armed. She kept looking down as David finished his wine and left the table. Her throat hurt, and she took another drink. She noted absentmindedly that she had a small bruise on her wrist from earlier. She wondered if she had one on her throat to match, and if she did, which scary man had caused it? *I prefer Jack's hand on my throat as opposed to David's on this strangely violent vacation*, she thought and bit her lip to keep from smiling in an absurd and frightened reaction.

Had anyone been paying close attention, they would have noticed someone listening in the dark. Just outside the now open door to the porch, the assassin was watching this scene unfold. He had quietly crept to the deck and hoisted himself to the banister surrounding the slightly elevated, screen-covered porch. Balanced on the rail, he had sliced open the side of the screen with his pocket knife and slipped though unnoticed. He peeked through the window and his eyes had narrowed as he watched Rebecca cross the room and give her shirt to the crying girl on the couch. He remained, hunkered down by the door. He could hear very little, but enough to understand they were currently counting hostages and missing one. From where he sat, one man briskly walked past him to cabin 11 and then returned to the lobby. They were looking for him. He watched them for a while. When he departed through the window to climb back over the rail, he heard a scream from inside. He returned and saw a man with his hand on Rebecca's throat. He raised his gun, targeting the offender until he released her. He listened as she lied. He knew they were not here for him. He suspected what they were waiting for was currently rotting in the back of a truck up the road.

He counted five men. At his count, two remained with the hostages, two by the road, and another that he had watched exiting the cabins. He recognized the two he could see in the lobby from breakfast, which meant he was missing at least one. They were six this morning. He had not seen number six yet. A minimum of six men, and he now had two bullets.

He slipped down from the porch and headed for the gift shop. Staying along the tree line, he quickly arrived at the shop and half-heartedly tried the door, expecting it to be locked. It wasn't. Apparently whatever happened here occurred prior to the evening closing ritual. The only lights in the shop came from the wall of coolers and a small one under the counter to light the wares. Most of the shop was as all gift shops: an assortment of small toys, games, T-shirts, and sweatshirts encouraging you to "GetAway!" hung throughout. Clothing, slingshots, rabbit skins, cards, some small food items, and other such novelties. He saw a small first-aid kit, no guns, and only a limited assortment of ammunition—none of

which would fit his .45. Along the back wall behind the
counter were a number of hunting knives. Choosing one
that was about six inches long with a hand guard, he slid
the sheath into his belt and took the first-aid kit, a black
windbreaker, hat, socks, pair of boots and a shirt with
him into the employee maintenance room.

Closing the door, he took off his now soaking coat
and dropped it to the ground. Using his foot, he shoved
it against the bottom of the door frame and turned on
the light. He stripped, and his sight adjusted to the now
blinding light in the small room. Seeing no lock on
the door, he glanced up at the small shelf next to the
sink where a screwdriver rested. He shoved that in the
doorjamb, took off his gloves, and examined his arm.
There was blood smeared from the injury all the way
down his hand, but it had stopped bleeding. He took the
same T-shirt he had wrapped around it by the car and
secured it tightly around the wound. He examined the
room carefully, cleaning up the few drops that had landed
on the floor and in the sink. He dressed in the clothes he
had found in the gift shop and put his gloves back on.
Turning off the light, he picked up his belongings and
took them outside, tossing them in the water. He very
slightly shook his head and his eyes narrowed again.

Heading back into the shop, he selected a bag from the
rack and began loading it with some granola bars, water,
and other nourishment. He walked over to the counter
and pulled a map off of the display, tucking it into the
bag. He also took matches, the first-aid kit, and a rain
poncho and shoved them into the bag. He moved toward
the back of the shop, returned to the front, and then went

again to the back. He did this a few times until he finally opened the back exit and looked off into the dark . . . and found himself uncomfortable.

For even the godless have moments of light. The assassin was having his first of these agonizing moments, and the sudden weight of it was terrible. Standing there in the doorway, bag in his hand, his eyes were fixed on a small, dusty picture that hung on the wall by the door. It was a picture of a dog.

Chapter 7

WILLIAM PRESSED HIS ear against the door, trying to hear what was being said.

"He was in another fight tonight."

"Boys fight."

"Not like this."

"With who?"

"Andrew."

"Andrew? Isn't Andrew three years older than him?"

"Yes."

"Well, it makes sense. He is angry. Many of our boys are."

"He's not angry."

A long pause.

"All right, bring him in. Let's talk to him."

William bolted back to his seat until the door opened. Inside, seated in an old, dimly lit office behind a giant desk, was Father Stephen. He was surrounded by papers and books, smoke hanging in the air from his constant cigarette. In front of him was a glass of whiskey, a book, and an overflowing ashtray. His head was capped with perfectly placed gray hair. He was clean-shaven and pressed, but still he seemed weary. Father Daniel, on the other hand, had a shock of red hair, bright blue eyes, and usually wore a bit of a red beard. He was a shorter man, well under six feet, stocky, and tenacious. Father Stephen had been in charge of the Saint Ignatius Home for Boys for the last ten years, and there was little he had not seen. Father Daniel was so much younger, and, although irritating at times, Stephen did his best not to extinguish his idealistic tendencies. He was a good man, just a bit too interested.

"Come in," said Father Daniel at the doorway. In walked a twelve-year-old boy. On his cheek was a large bruise accompanied by several scuffs and scratches. The knuckles on his right hand were torn and bloody, and his school uniform bore the appearance of a playground struggle: covered in dirt and ripped at the collar. The boy stood in silence.

"Sit down," Father Stephen said, gesturing to the chair in front of his desk.

The boy obeyed.

"So, you have been fighting again?" Father Stephen asked, keeping his tone calm and inviting. "What happened this time?"

"He challenged me," the boy responded.

"And so if you are challenged, this means you have to fight?" Father Stephen began his usual speech with little actual investment in the discussion. "Andrew is much older than you, William. He could hurt you. Fighting is not the answer. Why not walk away? Why not go get Father Daniel to help?"

The boy considered these statements briefly.

"Now he won't challenge me again," he said.

"What did he say? Did he make you angry, William? Did he say something cruel?" Father Daniel inquired.

The boy furrowed his brow in confusion at these questions.

"Yes, angry. Were you mad at him?" Father Daniel repeated.

"No," he said, with slight confusion evident in his tone.

The priests exchanged a glance. The boy sat unafraid. Father Stephen stood and went to the other side of the office, pulling an old metal first-aid kit from the shelf. He walked over and held it out to William.

"You are bleeding on my chair."

The boy picked up his bleeding hand from the chair and instead held it over his knee. He took the kit with his unwounded left hand and struggled with its weight and size to place it on his lap. The priests observed as he awkwardly fought with the metal latch closure with his left hand. Eyes down, completely focused, he continued to study the latch and try and open it. Father Daniel stepped forward to assist, but Father Stephen raised his hand and caught him with a glance, stopping him. William worked at the box for over a minute until it finally opened. He studied the contents. Selecting a bottle and some gauze, he opened the bottle and poured some of the liquid on the gauze strip he had removed. He closed the bottle and returned it. He then picked up the wet gauze and pressed it into his knuckles. As he cleaned his wound, he carefully inspected it, pausing to scrape out bits of dirt with his other hand. He took the strip and wrapped it around his knuckles. He then examined the arm of the chair where his blood had woven through his fingers. He closed and latched the first-aid kit, moved it off of his lap, and placed it with some difficulty on the ground to his left. He stood, pulled his shirt tail from his trousers, and used it to blot the blood from the chair.

Father Stephen observed all of this with great interest. The priests looked at each other in silence.

"That'll do, William. To your room now. Tomorrow after class, you come straight here, understand?"

"Yes, Father."

The boy left. The priests remained, considering the unusual behavior of this child.

"He was not the least bit afraid. Not of us, not of being in trouble, not of Andrew. Nothing," Father Stephen said perplexed.

"He didn't look up once," Father Daniel finally said. "He didn't look at either one of us, even when he couldn't open that. He never even flinched."

"Yes, he does not expect any help," Father Stephen agreed.

"He paid no mind to his hand," Father Daniel continued to make his case.

"How long has he been here?" Father Stephen wondered aloud.

"Longer than I have, so at least five years."

Father Stephen crossed the room to an old file cabinet. "I think since he was six?" Father Stephen found the boy's file and returned to his desk. "Yes, six. I remember now. He was left here. Father Harris found him asleep on one of the pews in the morning. Has he been trouble before?"

"Not really. Not until recently. Does well in class, high marks. Doesn't seem to interact with the others; he's practically silent. I think that's why he gets in trouble. The other boys, they don't know what to make of it. Actually, neither do I," Father Daniel said as he shook his head. He was a good man, a true priest, led by God to help the wayward souls of the world. This boy needed help. Father Daniel was only thirty-five years old, and he did not have the experience of Father Stephen, but he knew this behavior was not right. He had witnessed numerous fights among the boys there. They tended to focus on these signs of manhood. It was a point of pride, a rite of passage, or for some of the weaker souls, the chance to gain some attention. It was of significant importance to boys fighting to become men to have evidence of battle to that extent. This boy did not seem to care about any of that.

He also knew children looked to adults, right or wrong, to guide them. To help them when they struggled, to carry the weight they could not bear, to comfort and soothe the wounds a child alone could not heal. He was moved to help this boy. This was indeed his calling. William sought no help, no attention, and no comfort, and Father Daniel was intensely disturbed.

"We will keep an eye on him," Father Stephen said. He did not know what else to say. "You are right to be concerned. He is . . . damaged," he allowed. They both stood in silence a few seconds longer before Father Daniel took his leave.

William returned to his room. As he entered the barracks he shared with some thirty odd other boys, their chatter halted and silence fell over the room. He was becoming used to that. He climbed up into his bunk with his uniform still on and lay down on his back. Eventually, the others began talking again. He listened just enough to know that it did not concern him. His hand hurt, and his face hurt, and he was achy all over. He lay there awake long after father came and turned out the lights, instructing all to be still. He was just about to fall asleep when he was jolted awake by a noise outside. He lay there listening. It was a strange growling, whimpering noise coming from the alley behind the home. He rose, put on his shoes, and crept quietly out of the room to investigate.

He slipped out into the cold and moved toward the sound. In front of him in the alley, he could see a big, gray-speckled dog in the corner. It faced him and let out a sinister growl. He looked around and picked up a small block of wood that was on the ground. As he approached the dog, he heard Father Daniel behind him.

"William, what are you doing out here?"

"I heard something."

"Yes, me too." Father Daniel drew closer to the boy. He was still wearing his night clothes, but had boots and his coat on. Father Daniel walked back to the door and turned on the light to the alley. They approached the dog together and could see it had become trapped. Its front leg was pinned under a large piece of metal pipe that had likely fallen when the creature was attempting to gain rewards in the discards. It continued to growl menacingly at the pair.

"William, give me your belt." The boy obeyed. Father Daniel approached and knelt down next to the dog, out of reach from its terrible jaws. The priest formed a loop with the belt. "Stay behind me." William did as instructed.

Father Daniel moved slowly, attempting to catch the dog's jaw within the belt. As he reached forward, he moved too close to the dog and it latched on to his wrist fiercely, delivering at least two bites. William raised his stick, but Father Daniel halted the boy with the raise of his hand. The priest remained kneeling next to the dog, and after several attempts, he managed to catch the dog's snout and pull the belt tight, cinching its mouth closed. He breathed a sigh of relief and removed the pipe to free the creature. It had now stopped fighting, but was panting and letting out the occasional growl. It was completely spent. Father Daniel scooped up the dog and carried it to his room. William followed.

As Father Daniel held the dirty and bloody creature in his arms, he instructed William to take the blanket from his bed and place it on the floor. William put down the stick he was holding and obeyed. The father very gently placed the still growling dog on the blanket and examined its leg. He instructed William to hand him a towel. He wrapped the towel around the dog's leg to try and halt the blood. Before he rose, he reached out with his wounded hand and placed it on the dogs head.

"It's okay, boy," he said gently. He and the boy left the room, closing the door behind them.

Father Daniel told William to bring him the first-aid kit and went to wash his wrist in the bathroom sink.

The boy returned, placed the heavy kit on the floor and opened it.

"You do it," Father Daniel said. The boy removed the same bottle and gauze he used earlier and set about the task. He took the rag the father had been using to stop the blood and came forward. Stealing glances up at the father, he started to clean the bite.

"Not so hard, boy!"

He again glanced at the father, confused, and returned, gentler this time, to cleaning the wound.

"What is it, William?" Father Daniel asked, knowing the boy wanted to speak.

After a few minutes, it finally came.

"Why did you do that?" It was almost like an explosion, like something he was fighting not to ask, but had escaped anyway. "I mean, it bit you. Why did you help it?" he added.

While it was true Father Daniel was young and idealistic, and he lacked the years of experience and weathered appearance of most of the flock of Saint Ignatius, he was aware of two things at that moment. He was aware that this was the first question he had ever heard the boy ask, and he was aware of the severe importance of the answer he would have to give. He took the rag from the boy, who was still making a violent mess of his wound, and instead gave him the mindless task of cutting gauze. When William brought the gauze to him, he began to wrap his wrist.

"There are creatures, William, many creatures who exist on instinct only," he said gently. "They do not feel. It is quite sad, actually. They do not feel love or fear. They do not know joy or hate, peace or vengeance; they only act. They survive. This poor creature, for whatever reason, had become trapped. It was injured and cornered, so it attacked. It does not understand I want to help. You see? It does not know that it's all right; I have to know that for it."

The boy said nothing. Father Daniel knelt in front of him, looking him in the eye.

"And so I pick it up, I bring it out of the cold, out of the dark. I tend its wounds. I care for it. I do this because it is right, William. It is right to care for all of God's pitiful creatures. It is right to help them. I do whatever I can that it might learn love and peace. That one day it might learn that it's all right."

"What if it doesn't learn that?"

"Ah, but what if it does?"

"It will bite you again," William said defiantly.

The priest considered this. He waved his hand.

"As God wills."

The boy said nothing. He did not seem to understand this line of reasoning. What he did understand was that after that night, he never saw the father without that dog. From that night on, it walked with him at constant heel, in obedient and silent affection.

Chapter 8

IN THE FLOORBOARD of the truck, just outside the gas station where Janice lay crying and Officers Marcus and Kalo remained in handcuffs in the dark, the phone continued to vibrate.

"He is not answering," Peggy said in a near panic. "Why are you doing this? I don't know what else I can do. Please, don't hurt us."

Matt stood up and stepped outside in conversation with another man on the porch. They were now alone in the lobby.

"Why are they doing this?" Peggy whispered to the group.

"We have to try and do something," Rebecca said, ignoring the question. "They will kill us all." Speaking in hushed and rapid tones, she addressed the others in the room. One of the frail men who had been seated in the chair finally spoke.

"No. They said they won't hurt us. Just do what they say."

"They are threatening us with guns—they are lying.

They are not wearing masks. They are saying each other's names. They are going to kill us," she said again.

"But why?" Peggy asked again.

"There is no why. They are going to kill us," Rebecca insisted.

"Yes, she's right. We have to do something," the grandfather chimed in.

"Don't you dare, Charles!" Peggy said sharply at the grandfather. "Just do what they say."

"If something happens to me, you go with her. Understand?" Charles whispered to his granddaughter and pointed at Rebecca. He looked at her for agreement with desperate eyes. Rebecca nodded intently back at him.

"What do you mean, if something happens to you?" the girl asked and started to weep again. He put his arm on her shoulder, but he would not tell her it was going to be okay.

"Nothing is going to happen to you. They said they won't hurt us," voiced the same frail man. Charles ignored this and addressed Peggy and the others.

"She's right," Charles said. "They are going to kill us. We have to do something. There are four of us and two of them." He was not counting Peggy, his granddaughter, or the elderly couple. "You two, can you fight?" he addressed the two men across from him. They looked at each other and then looked down.

"I don't know," was the honest response from the first; the other just shook his head.

"We should just do what they say," the frail man said again.

"Yes, that's right. Just do what they say," Peggy hissed quietly from behind the counter.

"Be ready," Charles said, speaking to Rebecca. She nodded.

Matt returned. All quiet. Rebecca scanned the room, looking for agreement. All eyes remained down except for those of the elderly couple and Charles. They met her gaze with fierce intensity: *We're with you.* As good as that was, she fully recognized this would do little to help. The elderly couple appeared willing but less than capable to be of any assistance unless someone could give them a gun. She knew the same was true of herself. It was unlikely she could do any damage. Charles was a different story. He was older, true, but a solid man, barrel-chested with unwavering eyes. Beneath his pleasant demeanor and gray beard appeared to be a calculating and stoic mind most definitely capable of causing damage. She could feel it. The only problem was his granddaughter. He was, and rightly so, completely handicapped by his love for her, and therefore unable to freely act. She gave them both a subtle nod of acknowledgement, but realized sadly that if there were a fight, it would be theirs alone.

She was not angry. This was not their fault. She knew people often struggled with how to behave in unusual situations. Whatever survival instincts once existed had long been eroded by the influence of social grace. People now required training to respond. It was a fascinating aspect of humanity. It's one of the things that drew her to psychology. She remembered as a student seeing video footage of customers standing in line at a convenience store that was clearly on fire, case studies of people assaulting others because of a prank phone call, Milgram's obedience study, the list went on. There were numerous examples of survival taking the backseat to social norms or obedience to authority. People were no longer socialized to survive; they were socialized to comply.

She was pretty sure she could make a rapid exit out of the lobby and through the screens on the porch outside if the shooting started, but she would have to leave these people behind. Could she live with that? And even if she did succeed in making it to her car in the dark, she heard the boss say they were guarding the road. So, that would have to be the contingency plan. In the meantime, there was nothing she could do but try and be ready for an opportunity to act.

On the porch, Matt approached David, who was seated in an old wicker chair in the corner of the deck.

"He's still not answering," Matt said cautiously.

David did not respond. In fact, the only indication that he even heard this was a slight quick breath he expelled. He waved his hand, signaling Matt to leave. Turning to the other two men that sat with him, he said, "What do you think?"

"Maybe they are running behind," answered Jason.

"Could be they aren't doing it till tomorrow—that was the plan, right?" was the agreement from Nick.

"Changes nothing. We wait. Until morning if we have to. We will figure it out from there. You two go watch the road and send Ben and Vic back up here. Tell Vic to sit with Matt and the hostages and keep calling Kalo. Keep them alive. We may need to trade. Tell Ben I need to talk to him. I'm going back to the cabin." The men went off into the dark, each to their appointed task.

David returned to his cabin, but did not go in. He sat down and waited until Ben arrived. There was a reason he wanted Ben with him for the next conversation. Ben was reasonable. Ben was also fairly loyal as far as David could tell, and he was dreading the idea of having this conversation alone. Ben stood at about five feet ten inches, lean in build, and rarely angry. He did his job, did what David asked, never argued, and never questioned. Helpful qualities.

"I think we have a problem," David informed Ben when he arrived.

"All right."

"One of the guests is unaccounted for, and I think he might be trouble. It is possible he may be the guy they call the Poet."

"Poet?"

"An assassin." David sounded concerned. "We have to tell him."

They went inside.

"They still can't reach Kalo, and no vehicles have come by. Nick and Jason are at the road, and Matt and Vic are with the guests."

"Where is Kyle?" the response came from a man seated at the small table in the kitchen area. He appeared to be around fifty. He was only about five feet seven inches in shoes—short but stocky, strong-looking, with clean-shaven olive skin. His hair was still thick and solid gray, short and military-style. He had matching gray eyebrows over black and tired eyes. He had a cup of coffee next to him and a few maps open on the table in front of him.

"I asked Kyle to watch cabin 11."

The man looked at David, but did not speak. His question was obvious, and he expected a response. He did not tolerate stupidity. If you were going to run with Jimmy Buco, you damn well better figure shit out. It would not be spoon fed.

"Well . . ." David started, "we are missing a guest." David was frightened. He had personally witnessed Buco participate in the beheading of two different men, and one of them took a while. He had firsthand knowledge of his brutality. He proceeded, trying to sound as if he still had control of the situation.

"The name on the book says Jack Shelley. He checked in alone . . . but the thing is, he has a scar on his cheek." He waited for a response.

Buco sat up, looking carefully at David, and said, "Who saw him?"

"One of the other guests. Matt saw him too, but he left a few hours ago."

Buco raised his coffee to his lips and chuckled. "Shelley, huh?"

"Yeah, but I heard he was dead?" David added. "In New York? After that thing with Dicioli."

"That wasn't him," Buco said.

"Had the scar," David continued.

"Wasn't him," Buco said again with authority. He sat back in his chair. Ben cleared his throat, hesitant to speak.

"All due respect, I do not know what you are talking about." That was all he would allow himself. He wisely did not ask for any information, only felt the need to announce his ignorance. Any decision to tell him anything would have come from Buco; he knew enough not to ask. Buco and David exchanged a glance. Buco could see what David saw in the young man.

"You never heard of Anthony Lewis out of Chicago?" Buco asked. Ben shook his head. "I grew up under him, Anthony. A smart guy: very smart, and very ruthless. People didn't mess with him, ya know? He used to do stuff like invite you over for dinner and make you watch your wife give him a blow job—that kind of thing. One time I even saw him beat a guy with his own arm." Buco laughed and shook his head. "Anyway, he had a reputation that people didn't ignore. He was eccentric. It didn't take him too long before he had his own thing going. He was fair to his own, but if you crossed him . . . People feared him. Understand? He had a beautiful wife. She was damn gorgeous, Ben. Long, dark hair, body that didn't quit. Italian princess. Beautiful girl, and she worshiped him. Just worshiped him. And she was sweet too. Sweet girl. The kind of girl you can't wait to bring home to Mom, ya know? Anyway, it's probably been about twenty years now, but one day Anthony messed up. He had made a lot of enemies over the years, crossed a lot of people. He must have pissed off the wrong person because he and his lovely wife were killed in his home. Anthony was shot in the head, but not before he was forced to watch what happened to his wife. He had to watch this sweet girl, his wife, raped, tortured, and murdered. It was horrible, just horrible. You don't do that to a woman, ya understand? If you kill 'em, you kill 'em. You don't do *that*. I was there afterward. I saw the blood. She was naked, all cut to hell, beat. It must've taken a while." He shook his head. "Looked like he tried to get to her at the end. Crawled through his wife's blood to where she was, had her blood all over him. He died at her feet." He sighed. "Stabbed into the center of her chest was a book of poetry."

"The Poet," Ben said.

"Yep. Hired for a special request," Buco agreed. "Could have been anyone, really. A lot of people hated Anthony. The Poet had been there, and he had done the job. No one knows who this guy is or what he looks like, but he's around. Seen his handiwork a few times over the years. People say he's got a scar running down the side of his face like our missing guest. When you think about it, it don't sound too good. So stay sharp, Ben. If it is him, this guy is for real."

Ben nodded.

"Let me know when you reach Kalo," Buco said to David.

"I will," David said. He added, "It may not even be him." Jimmy Buco's face turned frighteningly angry, and David and Ben exited the room. Once outside, David turned to Ben.

"Tell Kyle to keep sharp, and then go sit with the others."

David sat in the chair just outside the door, gun in his hand.

Buco sighed. Stupid Jonny, getting pinched out here for some drunken nonsense, and here they were— waiting for a truck that was not coming and stuck in this godforsaken wilderness with no way to know why it had not arrived. Perhaps it was a last-minute change, perhaps they did reschedule for tomorrow, as originally planned. Perhaps it would show. Maybe this Shelley person was just another guest.

He was less surprised than agitated. Jonny was always in trouble. Ever since they were children, Jonny was the one that never learned. Jimmy, Jonny, and Jerry Buco. Their father beat them mercilessly, but to no avail. Jimmy turned violent. Jerry ended up being sent west with brain damage. And Jonny? Well, Jonny would do what Jonny would do. No amount of beating ever changed that. He remembered once when they were in their twenties, Jonny had become sweet on one of the dancers at the casino. What the hell was her name? Cheekie or something like that? Jonny was smitten, for whatever reason, and showered her with all manner of gifts. He even bought her a car. It was always grand with him. Two weeks after she finally agreed to move in with him, he beat her to death with an iron picture frame. What did he do then? He called Jimmy, of course, crying, angry, and drunk, asking for help. And what did Jimmy do? Jimmy took care of it. And so on and so on. That was his brother. Jonny would do what Jonny would do.

He got up and went to his bag. Opening it, he removed his revolver and placed it on the table next to him.

Chapter 9

"SON OF A bitch," Jack growled under his breath. He quietly left the gift shop and headed toward the light of the lobby. Staying in the shadows, gun in hand, he crept his way back to the cabins. Upon approaching, he saw the silhouette of a man seated against the rail at cabin 10, facing cabin 11. That must be number six. He knelt down and observed him briefly. Number six was smoking a cigarette, glancing around occasionally, but not with purpose. He seemed to be bored. Number six appeared to be intent on watching cabin 11. Number six was not watching anything else.

Jack holstered his weapon and withdrew the knife he had acquired at the gift shop. He adjusted it a few times in his hand, feeling the weight, becoming accustomed to it before he moved across the grass and approached number six from behind. He made no noise, and upon reaching number six, covered his mouth in a solid grip with one hand and stabbed him in the neck with the other. Six writhed in panic, struggling and swinging wildly, trying to free himself, trying to stop his blood. His struggling subsided after a few seconds, and Jack pulled him over the rail and laid him down in the bushes. He wiped the knife off on the dead man's shirt and searched him until he found his gun. It was loaded, but it would be loud. He tucked it into his waistband and drew back into the dark.

He returned to the lobby and pulled himself back up the rail to the smoking area. He knelt down, peeked through the window, and saw the scene unchanged. Each guest was still seated where they had first been, Rebecca still at the table. She was smoking. He could see an armed man seated behind the counter with the older woman, who was crying. The front door was open, and he noticed the armed man turn in the direction of the door. He appeared to be speaking to someone. He briefly remained, and then exited the porch through the screen and made his way to the road. As he approached, he slowed his pace and fell in behind the trees.

Standing on the road were two men. They stood, balanced, not slouching and not seated. They appeared aware, looking east. It was still raining slightly and very dark, with the only light visible from the resort and a couple of old lamps by the entrance. He had reached the end of the tree line, and there was nothing but thirty feet of open space separating him from the men in the road. He slowly moved around behind them, following the trees until he had no choice but to step out into the open. With his gun drawn and pointed at the man standing the farthest away from him, he stepped lightly toward them. They did not move, and they did not speak. When he was about ten feet away from the closest one, he shot them both in the head. After he fired, he dropped down to his knees and pulled the other gun from his waist. He did not need to use it. They collapsed in the road. He looked around and then walked over, grabbing them each at the back of the collar and dragging them off of the road into the dark.

Chapter 10

KELLY WAS A bit of a whore. Not necessarily in a bad way, but over the years she had developed a bit of a reputation, and this was certainly true among the boys of Saint Ignatius. Many of them had been summoned, at one time or another, to visit Kelly at her little one-bedroom apartment down the block. She was almost pretty at twenty-two years old. Her hair was strawberry blond, thick, and full down to the center of her back, and she had soft, white skin and light brown eyes. Her rough upbringing had created a sad figure, aged beyond her years. Although she acted tough, she was really an unfortunate creature, starved for an affection that was never quenched. She often sought to fulfill this need from boys down the street. For Kelly, much of her history involved cruel attention from lovers much older than her. She preferred the company of younger men. They were sweeter than men of her age. Always desperate to please, always lapping at her feet, waiting for her invitation. They were wonderfully eager lovers, even if they lacked a bit in the stamina department. She knew they would do whatever she asked for a taste of her wares, and in this respect, she had power over them.

A few years ago, she had met a quiet fourteen-year-old and, since then, occasionally invited his company. She had been walking past Saint Ignatius when she noticed him. Despite the fact the rest of the boys were playing baseball, this one was sitting alone, looking past the fence into the street. He had pale skin with dark hair and the prettiest blue eyes. Kelly said her hellos to her other admirers, but ultimately found him to be more interesting.

William was desperately quiet, most certainly shy, and no doubt intimidated by her advances. She liked that he had developed this quiet little affection for her, despite her being generally harsh with him. She knew he would come to her; he would sit quietly until she allowed him to touch her, and would leave when she was finished. He never failed to accept these invitations, and with her constant direction, he had become quite a satisfactory lover these past three years. He remained her eager student, and she did like to make him wait. Earlier that day as she strolled past the church, she waved at him and invited him over. It felt like a William night.

Kelly answered the door wearing only her blue silk robe, one breast defiantly visible.

"What they hell took you so long?" she barked at him as he entered. He did not respond. "Seriously, Billy, what's wrong with you? I don't appreciate you making me wait here all night. I have other people I could see, you know." She strolled past him to her dresser and lit up a cigarette. "I don't know why I even bother asking you over here if you are going to make me wait all night." He was always this late. She knew he had to wait until lights out when he could sneak out of Saint Ignatius. Breast still visible, she arched her back slightly, smoking her cigarette and letting him watch her. He stood in silent and hopeful remorse. She paraded around a bit more, picking up some clothing from the floor, moving the ashtray from one table to another, bending over to place her shoes in the closet. He did not respond. Finished with her usual routine, she strolled back to where he stood and put her hand on the doorknob.

"Maybe you should just go. I don't even think I feel like it anymore," she said and leaned back against the door.

He did not respond, but he reached for her breast.

"Billy!" she snapped, brushing his hand aside, but leaving her robe open. She tried to push past him, but he did not move. She sneered at him and tried to step away. "I said no!"

He stepped closer, his eyes holding her captive.

"Did you?"

It was like he had slapped her in the face. Looking up at him, she did not quite understand when he had gotten so big. He somehow towered over her. She didn't remember that.

She rolled her eyes and started to touch his face. He pulled his head back out of her reach, waiting for her to respond. She flung her hand down to her side with a sneer.

"Jesus, Billy, don't stop!" she said, rather annoyed.

His hand returned to her breast as his other hand pulled the sash on her robe, allowing it to fall completely open. His hand moved slowly, enticing, stroking between her legs. When she whimpered, he growled quite clearly in her ear.

"Tell me no."

She gasped in disbelief. Did he just say that? She kept moaning and pulled at his clothing, freeing him, encouraging him. As she grinded against him, trying to pull him closer, he said it again.

"Tell me no." His tone was not playful. His tone was not seductive. He spoke with a cold dominion, and he intended that she answer.

"No . . . oh . . . no . . ." Kelly became afraid. She started to tremble.

He took her then. He kept her against the door until her legs trembled and she clung to his neck to keep from falling. After that, he moved her to the bed and took her a while longer, until he was finished. As he dressed to leave, she curled up into a ball and pulled the covers tightly around her, looking past him out the window. She suddenly understood his shy and silent manner was not due to some remorse or intimidation, but something else entirely. She shivered, thinking of his tone, his other visits, his silence, him. She had the realization it was not that she lost the affection of this boy; she had never had it in the first place. She had experience with men who would visit just to use her body; this was different. Those men were barely present. He was aware of every single whimper, of every shameful moan. Kelly would later describe it as how an insect might feel when a boy has ripped off its legs and watches it struggle. Not watching with pleasure, but watching with an idle curiosity. What she refused to describe was how horrifically satisfying he was. How he made her scream in terrible ecstasy. She did not invite him back.

And such was usually his experience with women. They would approach him at some bar and sit with him for a while. They would misinterpret his scars for character, and his silence for interest. They would invite him in, and they would tremble. Afterward, as they lay there, or when they sobered up, they would draw their knees to their chest, pull the covers up to their chin, and wait, desperate for him to leave so they could lock the door behind him. They all felt it. That sudden knowledge they had made a horrible mistake. That something was wrong. That feeling that even though he chose to make them scream with pleasure, he could just as easily have made them scream another way.

They were right.

Chapter 11

B EN LEFT DAVID and Buco in cabin 1 and walked to cabin 11 with his gun in his hand. They were concerned about the identity of this missing guest, and Ben knew that meant he needed to be alert. He had never seen David that uncomfortable. The lights were on in every cabin, and all the doors remained open. As he walked past, he glanced in each room but did not see anything interesting. He walked past the lobby without speaking to Vic. When he reached cabin 10, he slowed and searched for Kyle. He peeked into cabins 9 and 10, and entered cabin 11. Finding nothing, he returned outside.

"Kyle?" he spoke into the dark. There was no answer. He felt cold. After a few minutes of searching, he withdrew, not seeing the body in the bushes at the base of the deck. He turned and quickly headed back to where David sat. He was walking so quickly that as he passed the lobby, Vic sat up and put his hand on his gun.

"I can't find Kyle. He's not anywhere," he spoke deliberately, and David stood up.

"Go tell the others and stay with them."

He then knocked lightly on the door and entered to inform Buco.

In the lobby, Matt was seated next to Peggy. There were four empty beer bottles on the counter in front of him, and he was indulging in number five. Vic sat just outside the door, watching the road, watching Ben approach.

"David said to tell you Kyle is missing," he said simply. That was, in truth, the only thing he knew for certain. Vic shrugged, unconcerned.

"He will turn up. He's probably sleeping somewhere."

"You ever hear of some guy called the Poet?"

"No," Vic replied, and thought for a minute. "Wait, yeah. I heard about him. Why?"

"David thinks he might be the missing guest."

"No, that guy's dead. He's been dead for a few years now, I think."

Ben remained standing, back to the wall.

Inside, Matt stood up and loudly set his beer down on the counter. He stretched. He walked over to the couch where the girl was sitting and knelt down in front of her.

"How you doing, honey?" he said, running his finger along the couch edge.

"Leave her alone," Charles said.

Matt did not even look at him. His eyes never left the girl. The others sat motionless. From outside, Vic saw Matt had left his post. He stood up and entered the room, taking the seat next to Peggy. He leaned back and put his feet on the counter, watching the TV that was on in the back of the bar.

"I said how you doing, honey?" Matt said again, louder this time. She did not respond but put her head down on her knees, which were still drawn up to her chest.

"Don't talk to her," Charles ordered.

"Maybe I should try and call again?" Peggy offered, seeing what was happening and trying to do something, anything to stop him from . . . whatever he was doing.

"Shut up," Matt said to Charles. "I'm just trying to be friendly," he said, placing one hand on the gun in his belt and running a finger lightly along her shin. She recoiled. "Do you know how to be friendly, honey?" he added.

"Leave her alone," Charles said again, more pleading than ordering. The girl was starting to cry.

Rebecca was watching all of this from where she sat. Watching Matt smirking up at the young thing, watching Charles contain his rage. She felt an overwhelming revulsion, knowing what would be next. She knew, *knew*, that if this went any further, not only would this girl be hurt, she would likely get to see her grandfather die in the process. They all might get to see that. A begging Charles bleeding on the floor as his granddaughter was pulled from the room, crying.

Rebecca decided she would not sit silently and watch this continue. She could not live with it. As things stood, she probably only had a few more hours anyway, and she sure as hell would not spend them in regret. A horrible coldness crept over her. A grieving. She blinked away a tear and lit her last cigarette. She knew this type of man. She had studied sexual offenders. She suspected his typology was currently along the spectrum of a power-assertive rapist. Exploiter of women. Employs violence and humiliation, and is prone to victims of opportunity. Insecure. This offender needed a confirmation of manhood. Rebecca knew exactly how to refocus him, if only temporarily.

She uttered a harsh laugh. The room looked at her.

"Seriously? What is it about a grown woman that you find so intimidating?"

She said it with the perfect amount of disdain, the perfect amount of mocking tone, sounding drunker than she was. Then she gave a small little laugh and added, "She's just a kid."

At first he only looked at her. She met his gaze and bore her mocking eyes into his. He turned just a bit toward her and raised his eyebrows in surprise, anger just starting to register. She exhaled smoke into the room without a care in the world. He stood and started forward, and she knew she had him. At his approach, she leapt from the table, knocking the chair to the floor, and backed up, letting him see her afraid.

"You say something, bitch?" he growled.

"I'm sorry! No . . . please don't!" she screamed as he came. *Yeah, that's right, come on, you filthy bastard. Let's do this. Let's see what you got. . .*

He grabbed her by the hair and jerked her head back against the wall. Peggy screamed.

"Okay, honey; let's see if you know how to be nice," he said as he was dragging her out of the lobby door by her hair. Rebecca heard herself scream. Charles stood up and yelled something she could not understand. The others sat, motionless—afraid. Victor did not stir but yelled back at Charles to sit down. Matt was shoving her down the deck to the far cabins, mostly by her hair. She fought some, but not fully. She was trying to focus. She was trying to get angry. Trying to find rage.

I am going to kill this man. God help me, I will kill this man. I will kill this man. I will. Come on, you fucking bastard. You want this? You think you want this? I'm going to make you earn it.

She clung to it, embraced it. If she was going to die tonight, then she would die. She would die fighting. She would die well. *You're just a man. Stronger, yes, but just a man. You underestimate me. I am a woman. I can kill you, smile, and then go home and make dinner. You predator. You rapist. You slow and stupid pedophile. And, oh yes, if you do win this fight, you will remember me, asshole. You will remember me.*

"You want to play with me?" he screamed at her, still pushing her along the deck, hand firmly clutching her hair.

"No!" she weakly replied.

"You think you want to play with me? When I'm done with you, I'll make her suck that old man's dick," he snarled. He threw her into the second cabin and slammed the door behind them.

Chapter 12

J ACK WAS MAKING his way back to the lobby when he heard screaming. Without consciously realizing it, he crouched down in the woods and slowed his approach. He finally reached the back of the building and climbed up on the porch and through the screen. The screaming had stopped. Looking into the room, he could see a new man sitting at the counter, relaxed, with his feet up. Rebecca was gone. The chair she had been sitting in was overturned. He scanned the floor for blood but did not see any. The others in the room appeared shaken. The elderly woman who he had seen at the gift shop was openly weeping onto her husband's shoulder, and the young girl was doing the same with the old man. He felt a slight chill.

He looked out into the night, listening intently. There was only silence. He briefly debated. He would have to enter the lobby, which was, well, complicated. Even if he managed to enter without alerting the armed man at the counter, he knew the others would scream when they saw him, not to mention the fact that the armed man at the counter had been speaking to an unknown person or persons outside. A silent entry from the porch was an impossibility.

He exited through the screen, dropped to the ground, and walked around the building to the front door of the lobby. Pausing at the corner, he could see another man standing at the door. One armed inside, one armed outside. As opposed to the man inside seated with his feet up, this second man had the appearance of being aware. He stood with his back to the wall, scanning the dark horizon, gun ready.

Moving at a tedious pace, Jack remained in the shadows as much as possible while approaching the door. When he was drawing close, a gunshot cut through the night from the cabins behind him. The man at the door turned toward the noise and saw him. He raised his gun while Jack sprinted forward and dove into him, taking them both over the rail and onto the ground with a thud. Screaming erupted from inside the lobby as the others registered the gunshot—Peggy louder than any of them, Charles on his feet. Even one of the frail men stood and started to yell. The hostages were starting to panic.

Vic stood up and raised his gun at no one in particular. "Sit down! Shut up!" he yelled.

His attention focused on his screaming captives, Vic failed to see the two men struggling in the mud below. Ben's gun had gone flying during their descent, and he was on his back, struggling against the assassin's blows. Ben wildly threw out his fist and caught Jack along the chin, shifting his balance slightly. Jack pulled out his knife and plunged it into Ben's throat, but not before Ben managed to yell for Vic.

"Hey!" came a yell from the doorway. "Let me see your hands! Now!" Vic was screaming commands. Ben lay on the ground, writhing and clutching at the knife in his neck. Jack, realizing he was caught in the crosshairs, slowly raised his hands and knelt to ground, eyes locked on Vic. He still had the gun tucked in the back of his waistband, but before he reached for it, Vic staggered to the floor. From behind Vic, Charles stood holding a fire extinguisher. Seizing this distraction, Charles brought the extinguisher down squarely at the back of Vic's head, several times. Charles kept raining blows at Vic's head until Jack made it to the lobby door. The hostages were screaming, but they were standing frozen, awaiting the outcome of this struggle rather than choosing sides. Jack put his hand on Charles's arm. He dropped the fire extinguisher on the ground in the pile of blood and brain that was once Vic's head. Silence fell over the room.

"Where is she?" Jack asked.

No one spoke. Everyone stood motionless at the sight of the assassin. He was covered in blood and dirt, wounds from his face and neck smeared in coppery black. He knelt down and began checking the pockets of the corpse on the ground. He picked up Vic's gun.

"Where is she?" he asked again, looking at Charles.

"I'll call the police!" Peggy screamed and ran to the phone. The assassin stepped in front of her and tore the phone out of the wall. Peggy recoiled and just stared at him.

"He took her. I don't know, that way. Please," Charles finally responded. He was panting and gesturing in the direction Rebecca was taken, having a hard time speaking. His granddaughter rushed to him and clung to his waist. Jack briefly looked at the girl and then at the others. They were all just standing there. He recognized they were afraid and waiting for his instruction, or possibly his permission.

"Thank you," he said to Charles as he handed him the gun he had taken off of the corpse. "Do you have a car?"

"Yes, we can take my truck, but we have to get the girl."

"I'm getting the girl. Drive to the second town east and call the police. The second town—got it?" Jack repeated. He was already heading in the direction Charles was gesturing.

The others were starting to respond now, recognizing it was time to move.

"Let's go," Charles said. The group followed him outside, the elderly couple moving as quickly as possible, the two men and Peggy assisting. Charles and crew started the treacherous journey to the parking lot. He was moving at a steady pace, but slow enough so the others could keep up. In one hand he held his granddaughter; in the other he held a gun. It was dark and slippery outside, and they were not able to move fast. As they approached the cars, Charles hit the button on his keys, and a large green SUV beeped and flashed its lights. They all piled inside. When they hit the road, the car began to transition from fear to relief. Peggy laughed a crazy sort of giggle, followed by the other men in the backseat.

Charles breathed a sigh and patted his granddaughter on the leg.

They headed east. Charles slowed at the two stop lights that were not functioning and continued.

"Here! Stop here!" Peggy said. "We can call from here!"

Charles kept driving. As they passed the town, the others in the car were yelling at him to turn around, to go to the brightly lit restaurant, or that bar over there! Charles kept driving. When they wouldn't stop, he said, "Shut up. Look, I don't know who that guy was, but he saved our lives. He said the second town. We're going to the second town."

"Oh, you mean the guy who ripped the phone out of the wall?" Peggy said, disgusted. "You're right! We don't know who he is. He could be one of them!"

The others in the car kept debating: "Who was he? Why did he help us? My God, did you see his eyes? Did you see the blood? Why did he tear the phone out of the wall? He was beat to hell. That was really scary."

Charles kept driving, and that eventually became talk of, "I can't believe we're alive. I can't believe we made it out of there. Do you think that girl is okay?" Tears came through laughter, and the occupants hugged each other and celebrated with smiles of disbelief. Charles's granddaughter leaned over from the passenger seat and laid her head on Charles's arm.

"Grandpa, I love you."

"I love you too, baby girl."

When they reached the second town, they stopped at a small diner. They were quite the sight, exiting the vehicle in pajamas, laughing with tear-streaked faces, Charles with blood on his hands and clothes. They entered the diner, and all were silent, falling in line behind the newly designated leader of the group. Charles approached the counter and asked them to please call the police. There was trouble at the GetAway Resort.

Chapter 13

REBECCA STUMBLED TO her feet, clutching the chair in front of her. Matt stood at the door, spitting out threats. The knowledge that she was going to die was slightly liberating. As she stood, she felt tears start to well up, and a couple slipped out. Matt smiled and came forward. When he reached the table, he pulled his gun and set it down, leering at her. The second his hand left the weapon, she swung the chair with all of her strength and caught him directly on the chin with the chair leg. He went back, flailing his arms to stop his fall, and caught the bottom of the table, flipping it up and making the gun slide down to the floor behind it. He did not fall. She came forward, swinging again, but he blocked it this time and came at her, grabbing her arm and wrenching the chair from her grip. He pulled back to punch her, and she managed to duck, avoiding most of the blow. Then he had her.

Holding both of her arms, he shook her violently, screaming, "Bitch! You fucking bitch!" Blood spewed from his mouth. He threw her toward the bed. She landed on the floor in front of it, struggling to get to her feet again. He was on her then, dragging her up by her hair and roughly throwing her on the bed. Her hands were holding his arm, trying to pull free from his grip. She hit him a few times in the face with her fists, but it did nothing. He got on top of her, holding her wrists over her head with one hand as she struggled. Less frantic now, he pinned her legs between his and stretched out next to her.

"Nice try, bitch," he said as he smiled down at her, blood on his teeth. "If you wanted to play with me, why didn't you just ask, huh? No need for all that." His mouth was on her neck. "Little whore."

He smelled like beer and blood. She felt nauseous, jerking her head to the side. His free hand went to her jeans, pulling at the zipper and opening them. His hand plunged down between her legs, invading.

"Oh, see . . . yeah . . ." He was crooning when he slid his fingers inside her. She clenched her teeth together, refusing to scream.

"God, bitch, you like that, don't you? Yeah. You like that. You gonna cum for me? You gonna cum for me?" His fingers were violent. Painful. She felt herself wince.

"Fucking bitch, you like it." He was getting more aggressive, wrenching her wrists and demanding a response. "I wanna hear you," he said, his mouth at her ear. He was panting. She could feel him pressed against her thigh. He was moving slower now, which made this even more repulsive. His tone was more controlled, more sadistic. She kept her head turned away, not looking at him. "I'll stop when you cum. Little whore, you're so wet.

Tell me you like it." His fingers moved deeply inside her. "I want to hear you scream. I want to hear you."

Fuck you. Kill me. I will not scream. I will not scream.

Still holding her wrists in one hand, his other hand slid out of her and jerked her top up over her breasts. He pulled down her bra, exposing her. His hand returned, and he was stroking her again. His mouth went to her chest. It was wet and warm, and she could feel either his spit or his blood start to drip down in between her breasts. She tried not to struggle against him. His mouth moved to her nipple, tonguing it viciously. Suddenly, he clamped his teeth down hard just over her left breast. Very hard. He tore at her, drawing blood and bits of flesh.

She did scream.

"Good girl." He smiled at her now with her blood on his teeth. "See, you need to just do what I want. You're going to anyway, honey. We've got all night. You like it in the ass, don't you?" He started mauling her body, hand roving up and down quickly, finishing with his fingers, almost his whole hand violently pushing inside of her, causing her to cry out again. "I know," he said as he roughly pulled her jeans down. She struggled again, feebly pushing against him and trying to free her wrists. He watched her with enjoyment and groaned. She fought him as best she could. She was kicking and writhing under him, trying desperately to break his grip. It was useless. He was far too strong. He kept pulling her clothes off until she was completely naked from the waist down. He freed himself, and she could feel him hot and vile against her side.

He straddled her and took one wrist in each hand. She

still would not look at him. She knew she had lost. She could now feel him on her stomach. The smell of him, the feel, him leering down at her. Again, she felt that she might throw up. The fact that he would have her was horrific enough. The fact that he intended to take his time . . . *Oh my God . . . no . . .*

"Fuck you," she said coldly.

"Hmmm . . . Don't be scared, honey," he said, looking down at her smiling. "I'll be gentle." When he said that, he squeezed her wrists really hard and sneered. He slid down her body, moving just over her. She felt him dangerously close, pausing where he could easily have had her. He pressed against her, but did not enter her. She was frozen, afraid the slightest movement would have him inside of her. "Yeah, not yet, bitch." He stayed there, his feet now on the floor, bringing her wrists down to her sides. He slid further down, mouth now on her stomach. He was licking her body as he spoke, saliva and blood trickling down her side. "Fucking whore."

"Fuck you!" she screamed. Her eyes were dry, burning not with fear but with hatred.

He stopped. His hand left her wrist and he slapped her hard in the face, starting to speak disapproval. "I've been nice to you so far." One hand now free, she drove her thumb at his eye.

"Fuck you!" she heard herself scream as she caught his eye socket and shoved her thumb in as deeply as she could. It was a disgusting wet and warm slimy hole. He shrieked and jerked back, hand over his eye. He let her go and stumbled backward, blood pouring through his fingers. She starting kicking and landed one heel on his nose. He screamed again. She pulled away to try and run.

He crashed against the nightstand, knocking over the lamp. He grabbed it and hurled it at her, screaming, "I'm gonna kill you, you fucking bitch!"

Rebecca took immense pleasure in the fact that his scream was now a high-pitched wail. She threw up an arm and blocked the lamp with her right forearm. Her arm felt suddenly warm and wet, and she could see it pouring blood, but felt no pain. He was getting to his feet, standing in front of the door. She ran to the bathroom and ripped the top off of the toilet base. When he followed her in, she turned and swung the heavy porcelain top at his face. It connected squarely and he fell down. She hit him again and screamed as a sudden and significant pain shot through her arm where the lamp had struck her. The base broke in half. She dropped it and stumbled over him trying to get to where she knew the gun was. He was still on the ground, sluggishly grabbing at her feet. She fell and started crawling toward the gun. She was vaguely aware she was still screaming at him. She kicked him a couple of times in the face as she tried to crawl away. He stopped moving. She stood and half walked, half fell to the table. She picked up the gun and came back to where he was, pointing it at him with trembling hands. He was not moving. She moved one of the pillows that was now on the ground over his mangled face and shot him in the head.

She picked up her clothes, dropped to one knee and threw up. She quickly rose and placed the gun down on the bed so she could pull on her jeans. She picked it back up and went into the bathroom. She did not look in the mirror. She pulled a towel off of the rack and wrapped it around her arm. She stumbled her way to the lobby as quietly as she could and saw it was now empty. Her vision was starting to grow dark, and she was shaking. She knew she needed to find somewhere to hide, as she felt she might pass out. She went to the gift shop.

Arriving, she went to the wall behind the counter and painfully turned around, leaning her back against it. She was still shaking, fiercely shaking, and could not stop herself. She kept the gun facing the door. It was dark. The only light in the room was from the display case. She carefully glanced around to see what might be in the immediate area that could be useful. There seemed to be blood everywhere: her shirt, her chest, her hair. She slid down the wall to the floor. She was trying to breathe deeply, afraid she might faint. She was dizzy, she felt a dull pain all over her body, and her arm was really starting to hurt. Still, above all of that, she was satisfied.

Chapter 14

AS INSTRUCTED, WILLIAM began to spend his afternoons in the office of Father Stephen. When he would arrive, the Father would have him sit at a small desk that had been placed there for him. On the desk was a book, which he was expected to read. There was no conversation. Father Stephen made no attempt at offering the care and compassion that Father Daniel tried to bestow. He considered William a troubled boy who needed to be removed from the others. Even more so, the boy made him uncomfortable. He would supervise, and William would read, and the days would tick down until he was eighteen and no longer required the services of Saint Ignatius, and that would be just fine.

At first, William struggled greatly with the selections. He had been educated, but not to the level of some of the classics he was expected to read. It took him a while to develop the vocabulary and the focus. At least once a week, Father Daniel would come visit him, always with the dog, and always under the watchful eye of Father

Stephen. Father Daniel would ask about the books William was reading, why he liked or didn't like them. He would talk endlessly at the boy about the moral code and characters of the stories. He tried desperately to take advantage of this time, to talk to the boy, to bring him out of his solitude, but sadly, the boy would not speak. He would only respond to questions and return to his book. Father Daniel always left those interactions wishing he had said something else.

After a few months of this, Father Stephen was called away to the hospital to tend to one of his parishioners. Father Daniel was required to keep watch on the boy. He and the dog arrived to find the boy again silent, again buried in a book.

"Hello, William, my boy. And how are you today?"

"Father."

"Father Stephen is at the hospital. Gives us a chance to spend some time together."

The boy said nothing.

"What is that you are doing?" Father Daniel asked. He rose from the desk and crossed the room, eyeing the task in front of William. "Oh, my boy, that is not right," he muttered. "I know there is a better work."

"Father Stephen has suggested it," William said.

"You can do better than that, boy," Father Daniel said. He pulled a dusty, leather-bound book off of Father Stephen's shelf and dropped it in front of William. It was a copy of *Les Miserables* by Victor Hugo. "Try this now," the father invited.

"I am in the middle of something else, Father."

"I know that, William, my boy."

"I am fine with that."

"Well, I am interrupting that. I want you to try this instead. Try this now, and then we will discuss redemption. It is my favorite tale."

"Yes, Father."

The boy did as he was told. When Father Daniel asked him how he liked it, he replied that he found the work uncomfortable. He appeared agitated when he said it. Father Daniel was deeply saddened by this response. He was troubled by the cold mannerism of this boy, fearing him irretrievably lost. Along with his visits, he offered a silent prayer for the boy at night.

After a few more months of weekly visits, Father Daniel entered his office. He greeted the boy: "William, my boy. And how are you today?"

"Father," came the boy's consistent response.

"How is your book, eh?" Father Daniel said, and continued, "I don't know if you know this about me, lad, but I used to be a bit of a boxer. Oh, I enjoyed that in the days of my youth! A good gentleman's match. Anyway, I have seen down the road that there is a gym. Nothing fancy, just a neighborhood gym. In fact, many of the men there have come through Saint Ignatius in one way or another. I am thinking of returning a few nights a week. Thinking of putting the gloves on again." William did not react to this but was eyeing the father respectfully, awaiting the point of this discussion. "I know I will be interfering with what Father Stephen has in mind for you—I am sure it is more than this—but I was thinking you would join me. Of course, it is not good for a young boy to spend all his time behind a desk." Father Daniel glanced at Father Stephen, who looked up from his papers for the first time.

"Why not?" he said. "You are right; the boy needs exercise."

"Excellent! William, we will start tomorrow after class." Father Daniel smiled and left. The next day, he collected William, and the priest, the boy, and the dog walked to the gym. This journey repeated itself three times a week for the next five years.

It wasn't the call of the gym that Father Daniel was interested in; it was the walk to and from the gym that he became most fond of. In the beginning, the boy didn't speak at all. The priest received more responses from the dog than he did from from young William. Slowly, however, the father's gentle persistence started to wear him down. It began simply enough: talks of the gym, the ring, tales from Father Daniel's youth. The priest spoke of everything he could think of, and occasionally, the boy would engage. He seemed to respond. He even started to ask the occasional question that was unrelated to boxing. After several weeks, the boy started to wait for him outside by the gate.

Father Daniel considered these moments small victories.

Over the next few years, William shared very little of his own thoughts and feelings, but appeared to listen intently when the father spoke. When he did ask questions, they were grand and unusual. They were more of a philosophical nature than typical daily chatter. His topics of interest were never minor. He seemed to have a high level curiosity about people, behavior, life. "Do you ever resent your sacrificial calling? Do you think Father Stephen does?" Once he even asked the father why he thought the other boys seemed to avoid him. Father Daniel explained as best he could that he felt they were afraid of the silence. William nodded thoughtfully, but never made any effort to change his behavior. The boy would only quietly reflect. He did not appear to mind the solitude. As a result, once when Father Daniel witnessed William talking to a young boy named James, he was inclined to inquire.

"What did you think of young James then?" the priest asked as they started their walk.

William shrugged and said, "Nothing."

"What were you talking about?" Father Daniel inquired.

"My parents."

"Your parents?" the priest echoed. "Ah! Yes, that makes sense. He is new to us. That can be hard, William. No doubt he wants to know. He has been asking about his own mother this week. Do not fault him. He is young. The curiosity of youth knows no tact. What did he say?" Father Daniel asked.

"He asked me if I killed them."

"What?" the priest gasped. "Killed them! William! What reason would he have to ask that?"

"They say that."

"Who?" Father Daniel demanded. "Who says that?"

"Everyone," William said simply. "That I stabbed them and cut them up. I thought you knew that, Father."

"William! You cannot think I would ever allow such talk!"

"Not to say you would allow it, Father. Only that you were aware."

"I was not aware!" the priest said with irritation. "You were six when you arrived here, boy—a bit young to slaughter your parents. True or not, it is hurtful, yes? To speak such evil of you! I intend to put a stop to it. Idle talk. I will speak to them about it. Tell them it is hurtful."

"They will not listen."

"I will tell them they are wrong," the priest continued.

"They will not believe you."

"I must do something. I refuse to accept it. I care for you, boy."

"Whatever you do, it will change nothing."

"William, I live my whole life to the contrary."

"You cannot save me, Father," William finally said. "Not from them or anything else."

"We will see, eh?" Father Daniel said softly. "Perhaps if I punish them. Hurt them back,"

"I did not realize priests were allowed to lie," William said. "You would not hurt anyone, Father."

"William, I am confused. Are you saying we should not hurt people for what they say?"

William's gait hesitated. He glanced at the priest with suspicion before resuming his place at Father Daniel's side. He responded, "I am saying you wouldn't."

"Ah! I see. I wouldn't," Father Daniel echoed. "That is no answer, boy. How will I know when to punish and when to forgive?"

"Do whatever you want, priest. Talk to them, hurt them; they believe what they believe. You cannot change that," William said with the tone of one who was done with this conversation.

"Of course you are right, boy. I would only change the deed, not the heart, eh? So the question becomes, when does one act on the deed?"

"Sometimes the deed is unacceptable," William said carefully.

"I agree," Father Daniel said. "Unacceptable, but not for the grace of God."

Such was the nature of their discussions.

The priest was well received at the gym. For the most part, the men there knew Father Daniel from the parish. He had been part of many of their weddings, funerals, illnesses, and confessions. Some of the younger men there had even grown up at Saint Ignatius, and although they were not raised with him, they knew of the priest and treated Father Daniel as if he were the pope himself. He was greatly loved.

Upon entering the gym, a type of alarm would sound where the others would loudly greet the priest with cries of "Hello, Father!" to alert one another he had arrived. At this point, all cursing, talk of women, and vile speech ended. Occasionally, someone would forget themselves and utter some vulgarity in front of the man. This was followed by sour looks from the others and shouts of apology. Father Daniel would wave his hand as if he hadn't heard and return to his training. Such was the level of respect for the priest, and so extended to the boy.

William was seen as quiet, eager to learn, and never a problem. The others welcomed him, but they were aware that there must be cause for such special attention from

Father Daniel. The priest taught him as best he could. He bestowed upon William all his love of the sport, the battle: two men, eye to eye, awaiting the bell. How he saw the savage grace between opponents as they danced. The patience of it . . . the determination. How sometimes one had to take a few on the chin and wait for the proper time to strike. To always be silently ready for an opening. Father Daniel loved the ring.

William learned to fight well. He was fast for his size, agile, and there was a fearlessness in his approach. Even when he lost, he remained steady and attentive to instruction. To engage William, one of the men would approach the pair as they trained and inquire if Father Daniel would like to go a few rounds. The father would pause thoughtfully and say, "No, thank you, but perhaps William would like to?"

At this invitation, the boy would stop working the bag or weights and say, "All right." Thus became the custom.

When he wasn't at the gym, William continued his evenings with Father Stephen. He would read in complete silence until the priest released him for dinner and then for bed. Father Stephen had recently arranged a poetry club in the group room in the back of the chapel, and once a week in the evening, some of the parishioners would come to read and discuss a particular work. Although William was not invited to these gatherings, he was forced to sit just outside the door so Father Stephen could see him. He would sometimes listen to the discussions, and sometimes return to his book.

As he aged and became more capable in the ring, he rarely lost. By the time he was seventeen, his skill was unmatched in the gym. Despite the welcome reception, he never really befriended anyone. He was not rude in any way, just quiet. He would acknowledge with a nod or response, inquire about a technique, but he made no effort for conversation. As he improved, one of the regulars there began treating him with slight hostility.

Richie had been coming to the gym just about every night for the past year. He was a decent-size opponent, standing six feet tall and proportionately built. He took little care of his own appearance. His mop of brown hair and unshaven face had the look of someone who did not bother consulting a mirror. At first glance, he presented an intimidating figure, but upon review, was considered to be more of a nuisance than anything else. He would train or spar for the better part of an hour, and then spend the rest of the evening wandering around and talking at whoever would tolerate him. He would talk endlessly about his whore women, his shitty job, and his overall superiority. When the gym emptied, he would cross the street to the local pub until the night was over and he inevitably had to return home. Actually, at twenty-three years old, Richie was always obnoxious, but only recently extended this quality to the priest and his ward. Richie had his own prior experiences with priests, and those priests were not as loving as Father Daniel. He had a foul and broken opinion about people that claimed to do good, people who were respectful, and a particular dislike for people who were quiet. He was not incredibly insulting, but he presented a harshness to the boy that appeared to bother everyone except for William. He would curse loudly in front of the priest, seeking out rebuke, to which he would reply, "What? It's a fucking gym." When William was in the ring, Richie would watch and ridicule, spitefully seeking an angry outburst that never came. Even the good father appeared agitated at times, but he would merely sigh and carry on.

Despite the tedium of Richie, the father was steadfast in bringing the boy to the gym Mondays, Wednesdays, and Fridays, come what may. Even after all that time, he was uncertain if he was having any influence, but the priest was determined to continue. To be honest, the boy seemed to get along with everyone there, always respectful, always willing to learn. He did not complain about anything. The fact that William never reacted to Richie's antics made the priest suspect the boy might be improving, but it also disturbed him. He was overheard to remark, "I am glad he doesn't fight anymore, but the boy should react to something." Not long after that, the priest received his wish.

The evening Richie approached was the same as any other. Father Daniel and William were working on the bag. Richie had recently lost his job. He had come to work intoxicated, and when his boss asked about it, Richie yelled at him. He was sent on his way. Still hostile from the wrong he had endured, he had been particularly surly that evening—insulting and vile to everyone at the gym. He had challenged everyone at there, but everyone had refused. Richie was too angry to spar with tonight, and he was irritating enough when he was still employed. Now he was unbearable. No one wanted anything to do with Richie, and Richie did not like to be ignored. He walked up to the priest.

"How 'bout it, Father? How 'bout a round, huh? I promise, I'll keep him pretty for ya," Richie said and winked at the priest.

William punched the bag a final time. He turned around, stepped up next to the priest, and smiled. He stood eye to eye with Richie, waiting for the father to provide his invitation. A silence fell over the room, and the others stopped to observe this scene and to look at each other. Father Daniel then noticed two of the men walking toward them. They had heard Richie, and they were walking with purpose.

The father smiled and said, "Oh, perhaps I will, eh? It has been a while! Oh, but I do not have my gloves. William, may I have your gloves please?"

William took a step back and turned to face the priest. He obediently handed his gloves to the father without a word. As the other men in the gym were exchanging glances to see if this turn of events was a satisfactory resolution to Richie's disrespect, Father Daniel was already stepping into the ring. They all took their places to watch. Even the dog, disturbed by the tension, rose from his usual spot in the corner and sat at William's heel.

The priest fought well. They traded blows and appeared evenly skilled, though each man was fighting a sporting match. There was no anger in the ring. Richie had been defused by the priest's obvious move to protect his boy, and Father Daniel was satisfied that Richie would not be harmed.

"Well, what did you think of that, boy? How did I do?" the father asked as they walked home.

After some consideration William said, "You fought

well, Father." Then he added, "You fought with the eyes of a warrior."

"You fought with the eyes of a warrior," the priest repeated slowly. "Ah, my boy, I forget your days are spent held hostage by books and poetry. You speak as such."

"That was my fight. I could have taken him," William said.

"Oh, you always fight well," the priest waved his hand. "No, it had to be me. Everyone was so angry. I was the only one I trusted not to hurt him."

"I wasn't angry. I would have fought clean."

"I've never seen you angry, William. Let's just say I didn't like the look in your eye, my warrior friend," the priest said gently.

"Everyone was so angry," William repeated. "You were angry?"

"I confess."

"I did not realize priests were allowed to be angry."

"I am human, and I failed," Father Daniel sighed. "He is a broken man. I should not let him get to me so easily. I should try to be an example for him. That I might teach him there is no cause for such disrespect . . . no cause for that filth. It is not for me to judge. Anger does not change the heart, lad; only love can do that."

"I have no concern for his heart, but I . . . You did not fail, Father," William spoke with total respect. For the first time in Father Daniel's life, he thought he heard affection in the boy's voice.

"I don't care for disrespect, William. I admit, I wanted to put the gloves on, but I fought without malice."

William said nothing. They entered Saint Ignatius and

headed down the hall to the barracks. William slid his coat off of his shoulders, down to his arms.

"Good night, William."

"Good night, Father."

As the priest moved down the hall, William slid his coat back up to his shoulders. He walked through the barracks, past his bed, and out the back door. He returned to the gym.

When he walked in, the men that remained looked at each other with a glint of excitement in their eyes. They acknowledged him with a smile, and he nodded a greeting but remained by the door until Richie saw him.

"Well, look who it is! The boy is back!" Richie sneered. He was standing in the ring, peering over the ropes. His tone became darker. "No father here now, boy. Come on up here. I've been waiting for this."

"The priest took my gloves, remember?" William said. He turned and walked outside.

"Oh, hell yeah," Richie said, stripping off his gloves and heading out the door. He was followed by the rest of the gym. They all filed into the alley. The men squared off, and Richie struck first, catching William across the chin. His second punch struck William in the gut. William took both strikes well and returned a punch, which connected squarely with Richie's jaw and took him to the ground. William was on him then, repeatedly raining down blows until he was pulled off of the bleeding man. Richie remained on the ground, moaning, as some of the other men went to his aid. William looked at the men holding him. When they realized he was not struggling, they released his arms. William turned and spit blood on the ground.

"See you Wednesday," he said, and then went home and went to bed.

The next day as he sat outside Father Stephen's poetry class, he could clearly see through the window an over-the-fence discussion occurring between Father Daniel and a couple of his parishioners. William winced and flexed his mangled hand. He did not sleep well that night.

The following day when the priest and the dog collected the boy, William made certain to keep his hands tucked behind his back. They walked in silence for most of the journey, which anyone would recognize as unusual behavior for the priest. They had almost arrived when Father Daniel finally spoke.

"Richie was in a terrible fight Monday night."

"I heard that," William said.

"Hmm? After we left. Not in the ring, though . . . in the street. The boys had to intervene. Had to take him to the hospital."

William said nothing.

"Well? Yes? Speak. Now what?" Father Daniel demanded.

"Now he knows not to disrespect a priest."

"Ah!" the father shook his head and put his hand briefly on William's shoulder. "I will accept that as a sign of your affection. Still, William, I do prefer you choose to fight in the ring."

"It sounds as if you are suggesting I did this," William said.

"I suppose it does. Well, whoever he was, I suspect it was on my account. What do you think?"

"I think there would be consequences."

"And so there should be. Beating a man in the street is not civilized. Although I will say, I am told whoever did that to Richie practiced restraint. I am certain this was on my account as well. I hope he will remember to do that should such matters arise again."

"Why?"

"One must always practice restraint, William. Especially when one is the superior warrior. If I knew who it was, I would tell him Richie needs a different approach. Kindness would work better."

"That seems flawed."

"Not flawed: forgiving. He held back, didn't he? My defender?"

"How would I know that, Father?"

"Are you going to tell me what happened to your hand, boy?"

"No."

The priest turned his head, but it was too late. William already saw him smile. They entered the gym, and they did not revisit the conversation.

At the gym, balance now restored, the others seemed to appreciate William's intervention. They felt it the right thing to do. They also caught a glimpse of why Father Daniel had taken such a special interest in this boy. His lack of emotion during the fight was unnerving. Still, they noticed, to his credit, that even when Richie did return to the gym, William paid him no mind. He had no need to repeat himself.

Chapter 15

IT DID NOT take Jack long to find which cabin Rebecca had been taken to. There were obvious signs of a struggle, and quite a bit of blood on the floor. He entered and saw that there was a half-naked man in a pool of blood on the ground. He pulled the pillow off of Matt's face and noted he was quite dead. He looked around the room, seeing the battle for what it had been. He saw the bed linens violently thrown around, saw the broken lamp and toilet base, saw the vomit on the floor. He searched the dead man's pockets, but did not find anything. His gun was gone. While exiting the room, he noticed small drops of blood on the deck heading in the direction of the gift shop. He ran there.

"Rebecca? Don't shoot." Jack opened the door but remained outside, speaking quietly from the dark.

"Yes," Rebecca said from inside. Jack quickly came toward her.

"Oh thank God, Jack. There are men here with guns," Rebecca said with tears starting to spill onto her cheeks.

He knelt down next to her.

"Hi." His tone was calm. "Stop crying, now. There are men out there. They are armed and looking for us." He sounded as if he were ordering lunch.

She stopped crying and whispered, "They were asking about you."

"They aren't here for me."

"Oh! We have to help the others. I don't know where they are," Rebecca said as she was starting to try and get up.

Jack placed a hand on her shoulder, settling her back down, and said, "They have gone to get help. Be still."

He examined her briefly, rose, and disappeared into the back of the store. When he returned, he opened a bottle of water and handed it to her along with two Tylenol. She drank down half of it. She did not even know she was thirsty. In the blue lights of the shop, she noticed he was carrying a bag and a shirt.

"Can you walk?" he asked.

"Yes."

He helped her up and led her to the maintenance room he had visited earlier. He closed the door and positioned the sweatshirt at the gap underneath before turning the light on. It was blinding, and Rebecca held her hand up in front of her face and leaned against the wall. She slid down into a sitting position. Fully seeing him now, she gasped at his appearance. He was covered in blood and dirt, obvious wounds on his neck and face, red streaking down his shirt. He moved as if he were uninjured. He glanced around, grabbed the screwdriver that he had used earlier, and drove it between the door and the frame. He turned and crouched in front of her.

"Don't look at me. Look at the door. Be still." His tone remained calm but very serious. "Where are you hurt?"

She held up her arm. He raised it gently by the elbow and examined the slash she had on her forearm. It was swollen and starting to turn blue.

"What happened?"

"That guy attacked me. He hit me with something. I think it was a lamp."

"I think it's broken. It is still bleeding." As he spoke, he opened a package of super glue and took off his gloves.

"Does that work?"

"It works, and it burns."

His grip tightened on her bicep and he poured water over her arm. He blotted it with a towel, and then she felt a horrible burning on her arm. Her body was reacting and trying to pull her arm away, but he held her there until he had finished. She did not scream, but rather let out a hiss, trying to be as quiet as she could. When she finally stopped struggling, he let go and wrapped her arm with gauze. Seeing the blood on her chest, his hands moved across her shirt to her collar. He ripped it open down the front and pulled off the bit that was now stuck there with dried blood. She winced, and it started bleeding again. He reached over and took the water from her. Placing the towel underneath the wound, he poured some of water over it, washing it off. She did not move. He was focused on her chest. He took the cloth and wet it, gently blotting the smear of blood. It was an oval shape with a bunch of small punctures and a nasty black bruise spreading out from it, oozing clear liquid and blood. He was cleaning it and suddenly froze and looked at her sharply.

"Is this . . . Did he bite you?"

This time she could not stop the tears, and they spilled out onto her cheeks. She kept looking at the door and nodded. She was finding it hard to look him in the eye. He was silent, jaw set.

"All right." He sounded softer now. "Do you want to tell me what happened?"

Still looking at the door, she shook her head.

"All right," he said as he cupped her face in his hand and wiped away a tear with his thumb. He took the bottle and dumped it over the wound a few drops at a time, catching whatever runoff he could with her shirt. She winced as it fizzed and bubbled against her skin. He placed a small piece of cloth over the wound and taped it there with the supplies from the first-aid kit.

"He didn't rape me," she finally said. "I shot him," she added, feeling she needed to confess.

"Yes, Rebecca, I saw that. I am sure you had no choice."

"I had a choice," she said quietly.

"Did you kill anyone else? The guy with the shaved head?"

"No." She was surprised at the question. His hands were moving over her legs and body, checking for injury.

"I told you, you would be the fight of his life. Are you hurt anywhere else?"

"I don't think so."

"The others have gone to get help," Jack said and put his gloves back on. "When they come for you, when they ask you, I want you to tell them I shot that man. okay?"

"Why would I do that?" Rebecca asked in a whisper.

"Just tell me you will."

"Why?"

"Tell them the man with the scar did it."

Still tearful and confused, she nodded. She chose to agree. She lacked the strength to argue with him right now.

"Do you have a car?"

"Yes, I have my keys, but they are watching the road," she answered.

"All right."

They heard the sound of the gift shop door closing. They stopped speaking and looked at each other. He pointed to the gun she had taken from the rapist and whispered, "It's loud." He stood up.

"I can try and help you," she whispered back and tried to get to her feet.

He turned around to face the door and stepped in front of her.

"Don't help me."

She was a fairly liberated woman, but not so much as to discount the severity of that moment. Being the weaker sex was the reality in her case. This was not entirely new to her. There were times at work when a particularly agitated patient would target her and start to approach. When this happened, the more agile of the security department would do the same thing. Step in front of her. Calmly, professionally, and with the sole purpose to prevent her from being harmed. When the violence settled, she always reflected with a small degree of wonder at the feeling this inspired. Granted this was their job, but it was not to be experienced without giving it the respect it deserved. The word *gratitude* does not fully explain it.

That simple movement that is so instinctual for some, and in reality so remarkable. To have him step in front of her that way created a somewhat indescribable feeling, a primal response: male protecting female. This was not his job, and these men were armed. Here, now, in the dark, he ordered her not to act. *Don't help me.* She responded with absolute obedience, full of fear and wonder.

He stood facing the door and removed the screwdriver. He switched off the light. Now standing, she moved along the wall to the farthest corner of the tiny room. After what seemed like hours, she could hear the door start to open. Jack forcefully pulled the door open, and the room flooded with blue light. It was David. She saw Jack step forward and repeatedly drive the screwdriver into the side the intruder's neck. Blood splattered out at an alarming rate, spraying all over the wall. She could hear it. It sounded like a sprinkler when it hits the window of a car. Jack wrestled the gun from David's hand and held him in place as he struggled to free himself. Trying to breathe, he was making a horrible gurgling noise. His face turned pale, and his eyes began to plead as his struggles became weaker and weaker. Jack allowed David to lower to the ground and started searching the dead man's pockets while he was still gasping for air and drowning in his own blood. It was creeping across the floor in a shimmering black puddle. Rebecca could hear her heart beating. She slid down the wall and pulled her knees up to her chest. Jack glanced at her and could see she was breathing heavily.

"Are you okay?" he asked, still crouched over David's body.

She slowly nodded her head, still caught by the dimly lit screwdriver slightly pulsating in the dying man's neck. Jack understood and stepped off the body. He dragged it through the blood and back outside the door, hidden from her view. He closed the door and replaced the now blood-soaked sweatshirt back along the bottom of it before turning on the light. Rebecca put her head on her knees and closed her eyes. Then she heard the water running. When he returned, his face and neck were clean. He knelt down silently and placed a small garbage can next to her.

"Look at me."

She did.

"I know that was messy. It's all right. Stay with me, Rebecca. Breathe; it's all right. Just breathe; you're doing good." He spoke patiently, tenderly. He handed her the water and nodded for her to take a sip. She did.

"That's right . . . good; just breathe," he said. She was as obedient as she could be, and the color crept back to her cheeks. "There you go." His voice had a tenderness she would not have thought him capable of. "Okay, want to try that again?" She nodded, and he helped her up. "I confess I had different hopes for this evening," he continued. "Were you going to let me in?" She recognized he was just trying to distract her. It worked anyway.

"Oh yeah," she said as she smiled softly though her tears. She reached up and caressed the assassin's cheek. "I was waiting for you."

"Yeah?" he repeated. He leaned in and kissed her quickly and sweetly on the mouth. "Let's go. I don't know how many there are. Don't look at him and don't hurry. You'll be fine."

She believed him. Each with gun in hand, they exited the room and the shop. She did not look at anything other than his back until they were again outside. It took a moment for her to adjust to the darkness, but he reached back and took her hand.

They slowly moved in the direction of the parking lot. It was all she could do to not run. A few times he had to pull her back, slowing her down. Agonizingly, they reached the remaining row of cars. He tapped her hand and motioned for her to start the car. She pressed the button on the keys, turning on the engine and headlights. It was the fourth one away from them. He motioned for her to wait and made no attempt to approach the vehicle, but she moved forward just a second too fast and suddenly felt the gun torn from her hand and arms around her waist and neck.

Jimmy Buco held her, gun pointed at her head. She searched through the night but could no longer see Jack.

"Step out here," came the order from Buco.

Jack stepped forward next to the headlights—gun drawn and pointed at Buco's head.

"It is you, isn't it?" Buco said. "Son of a bitch."

The assassin gave no response.

"Is he dead?"

"Yes."

Buco stood in silence, grieving his loss. She felt him sigh. She kept her eyes on Jack.

"I supposed it was just a matter of time. Did he say anything?" Buco added.

"He said he wasn't a rat."

"Yeah. He wasn't." His grip tightened on Rebecca as he continued, "Me and your little lady friend here are going to take a drive. Put down your gun." Jack stood unwavering. "Put it down, *Poeta*. No one wants another Betty Lewis, but you know I can do that."

Jack remained, gun drawn. Buco stepped sideways, closer to the car. Rebecca struggled briefly and Buco tightened his grip.

"You should be thanking me, honey. He doesn't treat women very well. Ain't that right?"

"Bethany," Jack said quietly. "I heard about that. Terrible death. Heard she begged to die in the end . . . Well, close to the end; she was a bit of a fighter." Jack smiled. "Beautiful woman. She was lovely even as she bled."

Rebecca stopped breathing.

"You know, I heard that wasn't even personal," Jack continued. "It was just a job. Still, sometimes a man gets to enjoy his work." His voice grew colder. "Can you imagine if it was personal? How she might have suffered then? And her spouse, her sons, her parents, her dog . . . her other brother. How's he doing? California, wasn't it?" Jack's gun never faltered. Rebecca felt Buco tense up. Tears slipped down her cheeks in horror at what Jack was saying.

"Put it down or—" Buco's threat was cut short by the bullet that pierced his brain. At that second, several police cars came barreling down the road and Jimmy Buco had turned his head just enough, responding to the sound of tire on gravel. He slumped down on Rebecca and slid to the ground. The police were pulling up, and she could hear doors closing and officers yelling *shots fired* calls as they took refuge behind their vehicles. She looked at Jack. He remained for a few seconds, looking at her, and disappeared into the night. She dropped to her knees. She tried to yell, "Thank you," but it ended up only a whisper.

"Hands over your head! Lemme see your hands!" someone screamed at her. She tried to comply, but could only raise one. It hovered there, and then everything went black.

Chapter 16

NOT TOO LONG after his bout with Richie, William began to notice a beautiful woman in Father Stephen's poetry class. As the evening would end, he noticed this woman often remained behind, talking with the father. Long, dark hair cascaded down to her hips. She was adorned with bracelets and rings, one golden cross around her neck. She had bright blue eyes and perfect skin. Her manner of dress was less than conservative, clinging to her body with an often plunging neckline and a silky material that wanted to be touched. Bethany was beautiful. She would remain and talk with the father. Sometimes after service, they would retire to his office and push William's desk into the hall. He would hear her laughing and moaning and would occasionally hear her shriek as Kelly sometimes would. He would sit there listening, often with a painful erection. When she left, she would smile at him. He would not smile back.

One afternoon, Father Daniel entered the office and told William to wait outside. Father Daniel was angry. William overhead the men in heated discussion, which ended when Father Stephen told Father Daniel his services would be better received at another parish. As Father Daniel left, dog in tow, he stopped to talk to the boy.

"William."

"Father."

Father Daniel stood in front of him. He forced a smile.

"My boy, I have been reassigned. I am leaving Saint Ignatius, just as you will be leaving here soon. You are a young man now, ready to go out into the world. I will miss you, my boy. I have enjoyed our time together. Enjoyed the ring, eh? When I get settled, I will write; maybe we can still go to the gym." Father Daniel struggled to put into words all of his feelings for the boy in the little time he had left. "You will be all right," he said softly. "William, try and remember to be gentle, eh? Be gentle. I will miss you, my boy. I love you." The priest opened his arms to hug the young man, but William did not move. He just looked at the priest. Father Daniel placed one hand on William's shoulder. The boy seemed to flinch at the weight of it. Father Daniel stood his ground. William turned his eyes to the ground, stepped in, and embraced the priest. He did not let go until Father Stephen called for him to return to his book. Father Daniel left.

Bethany continued to visit Father Stephen, and William continued to hear her lovely little gasps from behind the door. This went on for a few months until one day the noises he heard from behind the door almost forced him to again press his ear against the wood. It began with the typical moans he looked forward to, but after a while became something else entirely. It sounded like she was crying. He was just about to get up when the door flung open and Bethany ran past, tears streaming down her face. He watched her leave and returned to his book. He was now reading the *Art of War*. After about an hour, he was called into Father Stephen's office.

"Shut the door and sit down, William." Father Stephen appeared distraught. He also sounded drunk. William sat. Father Stephen filled another glass and handed it to the boy. He then offered him a cigarette. William cautiously accepted both.

"You are going to do something for me," the priest said. "This woman, Bethany, you have seen her, the one that comes to my class. She is in trouble, William. She needs our help. She has been unfaithful. Understand? Her husband, you see, he is a very violent man. This woman, she is in fear for her life. I think you can help her. Do you want to help her, William?"

The boy gave no response.

Father Stephen took another drink and lit another cigarette. William noticed his hand was trembling.

"There are men that you cannot reason with, cannot talk to. Her husband, he is like that. He will surely kill her. It is a shame. She is such a beautiful girl. You might be able to make sure that doesn't happen. He is an evil man, William, and even the Holy Father would agree that he deserves to die. Understand? And think about how grateful she would be to a young man such as yourself! I am sure she would be so very appreciative, William. You have seen her, yes? Think about that. I am sure you could sort that out with her." The priest emptied his glass. William said nothing.

"I could pay you two thousand dollars as well! Imagine what you could do with that money. I mean, you will be eighteen next month and have nowhere to go. You have a chance to help someone, a chance to do God's work, and get something for yourself too." The priest opened the drawer of his desk, removed a revolver, and laid it on the table in front of the boy. "Do you have gloves? Do you know how to use this? You need to be close, okay? You need to make sure he is dead. Oh, and, William, you need to make sure he has a chance to make peace with God first."

William finished his drink, stood, and picked up the gun. He fiddled with it until he opened the cylinder and saw it was loaded. He then reached over and picked up the pack of cigarettes in front of Father Stephen. In the depth of his heart, the priest knew the likely outcome of this decision would be that he would not see William again, but that William would be mistaken for her lover. The priest refused to hear it. The boy was young, after all. He was adaptable. The father would provide him penance, the boy would be forgiven, and sweet Bethany might live.

"Where?" William asked as he eyed the father coldly from across the desk.

The father sat bewildered. The boy didn't even argue with him. He didn't hesitate. In a trance, in disbelief that he had come to this, that he was somehow having this conversation, Father Stephen pulled a card from his desk and handed it to William.

"God's work?" William said, still facing Father Stephen. "Do you want me to make him watch, Father?"

Father Stephen was horrified. He opened his mouth to speak, but found he could not reply.

"I don't want your woman, priest."

The boy left. The priest threw up.

At around midnight William approached the house. The night was growing colder, and he paused at the window; looking in, he could see nothing. The house appeared to be empty. Moving cautiously around to the back, he tugged at the sliding doors and windows until he found one that was unlocked. As he pulled it open, he could hear a woman screaming. He froze, feeling a chill run over him. He entered the home and closed the door behind him. The screaming continued. He followed the noise until he arrived at what he took to be the entrance to the cellar. He did not have to worry about making any noise; the screams from this woman far surpassed any need to be quiet. He cracked open the door and descended the staircase. When he could see, he crouched down and stayed still.

He saw the woman, Bethany. Her hands had been bound. She was lying on her back on a table. Her face was swollen and black and blue. She was almost completely naked, clothed only in a tattered black bra and her gold crucifix. Her body, which had been beautiful, was now bruised and broken, streaked with blood. She lay panting, crying, begging.

"No, Anthony, please stop, please don't. I didn't do anything, please don't . . ." Over her stood a large man, shirtless, smoking, and covered in sweat from what he had been doing to her down there in the cellar.

"Who?" he screamed. When he spoke, he held up a

box cutter and sliced her across her stomach. Blood spilled out, and she screamed again.

"No . . . please . . . no!" she was begging him. "I love you, Anthony . . . only you . . . please!"

"Lying bitch," he growled. He cut her again. He began hitting her. He hit her mercilessly on her face and stomach. She kept begging him to stop. He started to rape her. She was crying.

Even if he had chosen to act, William did not have a clear shot. If he were to move, he would be seen. Although distracted, Anthony was facing the stairs. She continued to beg, and he abused her violently. He was slicing her arms and legs with the blade, sometimes hitting her with his fists as he moved, calling her a lying whore. He raped her for a while. The blood from her wounds was pooling around the floor and covering Anthony's chest and face as he worked on her. Finally, he collapsed on top of her. She was still crying. As he lay there panting, he cut her slowly and deeply on her chest. She screamed even louder, pleading with him to stop, begging him to not hurt her, crying, writhing against the ropes holding her down. He ran his mouth across the blood on her breasts and told her sweetly that she would die tonight. He moved out of view, and William crept forward. Anthony returned holding a book, reading aloud to her.

"Say the pagans: We were all born unlucky! The evil day has dawned for us today!"

Anthony paused and turned over the book, looking at the cover.

"What is this shit? Huh? *Poetry. This* is what you like?"

He struck her again. "What man of flesh and blood can ever hope to bring him down?"

As he read, he would occasionally cut her again, on her once beautiful legs, across her tear-streaked face, along her lovely breasts, this time with a large knife. She was begging him to let her live. Then she started to beg him to let her die. He finished reading. He opened the book across her chest and drove the knife down through the book and into her heart. She briefly struggled and then collapsed. Anthony stayed there, rubbing his hand along her inner thigh and his face along the blood on her stomach. After a while he moved to the couch and sat down. He was still panting and now faced away from the stairs. He lit a cigarette.

William crept forward with the gun. It felt heavy. He noted with interest that Anthony seemed entranced and exhausted. He was holding the box cutter again, unmindfully clicking the blade up and down. He was mumbling to himself.

"The pagans say we are all born unlucky," Anthony said and let out a chuckle. William raised the weapon to Anthony's head, and he moved in front of the couch to face him. Anthony looked up, somewhat surprised.

"Ha! You him, boy? You are too late. That bitch is dead."

William did not respond.

"You're going to shoot me now? She's been fucking everything that moves, kid. Not just you and me. Everyone! You should have spoken up—you could have had a turn. Lying bitch. Didn't know she was such a screamer."

William still did not respond, and he kept the gun pointed at Anthony's head. His hand was starting to tremble.

"Well, last request then, kid?"

"All right."

"Let me finish this smoke," Anthony said mockingly.

"I'm supposed to make sure you make your peace with God," William said.

"Yeah? Peace with God, huh?" the dead man said, chuckling. He sat there smoking, covered in blood and laughing like a maniac. "Well, let me think about it. How can you ever really know that?" he laughed again. "Oh, I suppose I have made my peace with the almighty. Why not?"

As he leaned forward and put out his cigarette, Anthony lunged, bringing the box cutter down in a wild sweeping arc in front of him. William pulled the trigger three times as he leapt backward out of the reach of the blade—well, most of the reach of the blade. Anthony staggered and collapsed, landing at first on his dead wife and then slumping to the floor in front of her. He crawled about a foot and then stopped.

William found that he was on the floor. He sat up and pointed the trembling gun at Anthony until he was sure he would not move again. He stood up, still shaking, and felt the room was growing darker and he was covered in sweat. He looked down at his shirt, feeling it was wet, and realized it was not sweat, but blood. He then realized he could not see out of his left eye. He felt panic creeping in. He put his hand up on his face, trying to stop the blood, until he found an old shirt, which he pressed against the wound. He went up to Bethany. Her eyes were still open and still looked frightened. In one of her hands she clutched a strand of white rosary beads. He ran his finger across the white strand of beads and then pulled briefly at the knife in her chest. She did not stir.

He sat down where Anthony had been sitting. He sat there for quite some time, holding the shirt against his face, breathing heavily and trying to calm himself. After he felt steady, he went up to a dusty mirror sitting on the floor in the cellar. He examined his wound and cleaned the blood from his eye until he could thankfully see again. Noticing that his chest was bleeding more severely than his face, he tried to put more pressure on the deeper wound. He returned to the couch and smoked a cigarette, looking at the woman splayed out on the table covered in blood, looking at the man he had killed. He was trying to slow down, to resist an overwhelming and incredible urge to flee the cellar.

Eventually, when he was calmer, he realized he had not worn gloves as the father instructed. He found another rag and started to clean. He wiped down the knife, the stairs, the beads, the door—anywhere he may have touched. He picked up the box cutter and put it in his pocket. He was unable to tell his blood from the rest of the blood in the room. Finding some bleach, he dumped the whole gallon over the pools of blood on the basement floor. He stayed until he was certain he had left nothing behind. Retracing his entrance, he exited the home carefully, closely watching that he did not leave any drops of blood. He did not see any. William returned to the priest.

Father Stephen, either too drunk or too fearful to bring William to the hospital, set about caring for the boy's wounds. After he made the boy drink a decent amount of whiskey, he took out his field kit and stitched up his chest. It was considerably easier after William passed out.

It was an emotional funeral service, this poor couple, killed in their home and with such savagery. Father Stephen, pale and trembling, performed the eulogy. Much was said about the horror poor Bethany "Betty" Lewis had endured, tragically while her husband was forced to watch. The parish was stunned. William did not attend. However, as he watched from his window, he noticed in attendance a number of men he had never seen before in the church. These men wore expensive suits, stood in the back, and were not received by those present to pay their respects. They were curious about the savage execution of such a powerful man. In the hours following the service, one of them sought out the priest, knowing he taught poetry, knowing he heard confession, suspecting he knew the identity of the assassin.

"Who's the poet, Father?" the man whispered to the frightened priest.

Father Stephen revealed he suspected the boy, and the fact that he was no longer a resident at Saint Ignatius. He was aware it was only a possibility William might kill him. It was a certainty that these men would. Although he had not seen the boy since he left, he did offer some suggestions of how to find him that were well received. Ruthless men in expensive suits appreciate certain skills. Not long after the funeral, William was offered his second job.

He had gone to get breakfast. The little room he rented after leaving Saint Ignatius did not have a kitchen. William had taken to going to the diner down the street for most of his meals. He was now fully recovered, though the wound on his face was severe. He had considered that he would need to have an explanation for that, but soon learned that no one ever asked. It was significant enough that no one felt it appropriate.

He was seated in his regular booth, reading the paper and having coffee. He was actually looking for work when he felt someone was watching him. He glanced up at the stools by the counter and noticed a large man seated there. When William looked at him, he rose and approached the booth. He stood respectfully until William nodded for him to sit.

He was only slightly smaller than William, and maybe about twenty years older. His hair was short and black, cut close to his head. His eyes were dark brown and set very close together atop his slightly pointy nose. He was wearing slacks and a shirt and tie with a jacket. He gave the overall impression of a weasel, but there was definitely intelligence behind that gaze.

The waitress came and refilled their coffee as they eyed each other.

"I thought you'd be older," the weasel said. William did not respond. The weasel sipped his coffee and kept eyeing William, looking closely at the angry red gash running down his face. "You looking for work, kid?" Weasel added, seeing the classifieds on the table.

The waitress reappeared with breakfast and placed it in front of William.

"You want something, hun?" she asked.

"No, thank you," Weasel said and smiled at her.

William began eating. The weasel reached across the table and pulled the newspaper over. He idly flipped through the pages.

"Just so you know," Weasel said, "no love lost there with Anthony. Business is business. His successor has made it clear we can't find the man responsible. No one's looking." William glanced up at him. "As far as work, I don't think there's anything in here for you, kid—not in the classifieds, anyway. I've got some good work available . . . something a little more poetic, I guess you'd say." William continued to eat. "Easy job. Two thousand. Half now, half later." Weasel ripped a piece of the newspaper off and scribbled on it. He slid it across the table. William looked at it, picked it up, and put it in his pocket.

"Five," William said and continued to eat.

Weasel paused and smiled.

"Five. Within a week." He stood and pulled an envelope out of his pocket. He placed it on the table in front of William. He knocked lightly on the newspaper. "Keep an eye on the personals, kid." He walked out of the restaurant. William continued to eat until the weasel was gone. Then he put down his fork and exhaled. He took a few deep breaths. With one hand, he opened the flap of the envelope and considered the money inside. He put his head down for a moment. Then he picked up the envelope, put it in his pocket, and finished his breakfast.

Chapter 17

REBECCA WOKE UP in the hospital.

"How are you feeling?" asked a young nurse who was tending to her IV pump.

"Umm, what's going on?" Rebecca was confused. She now had a full cast on her arm, and all around the room, she saw flowers everywhere. Flowers, balloons, cards, even a stuffed bear.

"She's awake," the nurse yelled out the door and came back to her bedside.

"I'm Sue," the nurse said. "I'm going to take good care of you, Rebecca. Don't worry." She spoke with such kindness that Rebecca was instantly calm. "You're in the hospital. You're safe now. We had to do surgery to repair your arm. Is there anyone we can call for you?"

"Um, no. I don't really have any family left," she answered, still a bit dazed.

"Are you in any pain?"

"Some. Where did all these flowers come from?"

"I will get you something to help. On a scale of one to ten, where would you say your pain is?"

"Four. Where did all these flowers come from?"

"Oh! You don't know? You are all over the news, girl," the nurse responded and turned on the television over the bed. Rebecca saw news reports flashing across the bottom of the screen—nine dead, police seeking information. She then saw an artist composite sketch of Jack on the screen. It was a slight likeness—not exactly right, but close. They certainly nailed his eyes. She then saw the grandfather being interviewed. His name was Charles Hayman. He was calling her a hero and naming Jack one as well. Police were offering a reward for any information and hoping the man would come forward. The female involved was being treated for injuries sustained during the incident. "Police are still hoping to speak with her as she recovers," the reporter said.

There was a knock at the door. Rebecca saw her visitor was a man of the cloth, no doubt making his rounds. His hair and beard were pure white, and his face held a pleasant smile.

"I heard you are awake. May I come in?"

"The police want to speak to you also," her nurse reminded her.

"God comes first, child." At this comment, Rebecca and the nurse smiled at each other. "How are you feeling?"

"Please come in," Rebecca said and shut off the television. He entered and sat on her bed, smiling gently at her. "I feel okay. Thank you."

"And what faith are you?"

"Christian."

"Ah! You know there is a God?"

"Oh, yes."

"Of course you do! You are his servant! Do you need any services today? Something to read, perhaps?"

"No, thank you."

"I should like to pray with you. May I?"

"Of course."

He took her hand between his and bowed his head.

"Our heavenly Father, I come to you this day in glorious thanksgiving! I thank you for your gift of this woman, and for the blessing you have given me in meeting her. I thank you for your mighty hand that guides us to find the light, even in the coldest darkness. I thank you for giving her strength during this time of fear. I thank you that you have crafted one so tender to call to save your child, so broken and so lost. I ask for your healing and grace for her, and that all that know her might feel your peace and love. Amen." He opened his eyes and patted her hand. She burst into tears and clung to his neck. She sobbed against him. *Yes, it was terrible. Yes, I was afraid. Yes, he shamed me. Yes, he hurt me. Yes.* He received her tears with kindness, putting his arms around her and patting her back. He did not move until she was done.

"It's all right, my dear. It must have been very frightening, very frightening indeed. I *am* blessed to know you," he said again and smiled. He stood to leave the room as she was drying her tears, not able to speak. When he reached the door, he turned and said, "Oh! I forgot!" He took a single red rose from his coat and placed it on the table. "From an admirer." He walked out of the room. She looked at the rose.

"Wait!" She tried to catch him, but her voice failed. She was crying again. She heard her nurse at the door telling someone that she was not ready to see anyone right now. She delivered the line with the fierce protective tone of a nurse who would absolutely not let you bother her patient. Rebecca gestured to the rose. The nurse retrieved it and handed it to her. She held it until she stopped crying.

"Okay. I can talk to them now," Rebecca said.

Her nurse briefly exited the room and returned with two gentlemen dressed in suits. They extended their cards and pulled up a couple of folding chairs closer to her bed.

"How are you feeling?" one of them asked.

"I feel okay."

"I am Detective Saunders. This is Detective Lance. Can you tell us what happened?"

She relayed the story—well, most of the story—of what had happened to them at the GetAway Resort. She left out as much information about Jack as possible.

"There is one Charles Hayman who insists you are a hero. That you prevented the sexual assault of his granddaughter by one of your captors?" Saunders asked.

Rebecca winced and said, "Any woman would have done that. She was just a child. I was pretty sure I was going to die anyway." She stopped talking.

"It appears from the manner of death he was no longer a threat when he was killed. Can you tell us what happened?" Detective Lance asked.

"I'm sorry, I don't really remember much. I remember he was beating me, broke my arm, took a bite out of my chest. I remember being certain he was going to kill me," she said and shook her head. "Then I remember waking up in the gift shop with that man."

"Who killed him?" Lance continued.

"It must have been him. Jack." A tear crept into her eye.

"And what do you know about him?" Saunders asked.

"He was the man in the cabin next to mine."

Detective Saunders pulled a sheet from his jacket pocket and placed it in front of her. "Do you recognize any of these men?" Saunders asked.

Rebecca could see a photo lineup of several men, each one with similar features to Jack. Blue eyes, brown hair, small facial scars on all of them. She studied it. It was old. The men were young, much younger than Jack. One of them looked like it might be him, but she couldn't be sure. It wasn't the best likeness.

"I'm sorry, Detective. Not really. Maybe this one?" She pointed at one photo as she handed the sheet back to him. He put it back in his pocket and instead showed her the same composite sketch she had seen on the television.

"Is this him?" Saunders pressed.

"It does look like him. Is he okay?"

"We have some information you two were close? You were seen walking together."

"No, I only met him that night. We did walk to the gift shop. He took care of me after . . . my injuries I mean. I was kind of out of it; I don't really remember too much of that. He put super glue on my arm. I remember that really hurt."

The two detectives looked at each other, and Saunders responded.

"He is currently unaccounted for. I believe he is a dangerous individual, responsible for the death of a person in police custody and the assault and attempted murder of three other individuals, two of them police officers. He is suspected in the death of the seven at the resort, and quite a few unsolved homicides. He is also wanted in questioning for the rape, torture, and murder of at least one woman. A hired gun."

"Rape and torture?" she repeated. "You mean he killed . . . *all of them*?"

Again they looked at each other.

"We were hoping you could tell us. We only have witnesses to one, and they maintain he was attempting to save them," Detective Lance said.

"I don't know. I didn't see that. I remember he told me the others had gone to get help. He was helping me to the car, and I saw the police were there, and then I guess I passed out. I don't remember anything after that," she said, sounding wearier than she was.

"Why don't you rest now, Ms. Paige. You have been through quite an ordeal. We can talk more when you are feeling better. In the meantime, if you think of anything else, or if you do hear from this man, you need to call us. He is dangerous. Understand?"

"I understand," she said quite truthfully. They left.

The next few weeks of her recovery involved multiple other police interviews with Detective Saunders, where she relayed the same story. He pressed her repeatedly about Jack. She explained she did not know who he was, that he had saved her, and she did not know why. Saunders was kind. He believed her. He also shared more unpleasant things about Jack.

She tried to do her own research. Who was this man,

really? What had he done? Could this really be true? She was unable to locate anything by searching his name. Although she could remember in specific detail every single word Jack had spoken, she could not remember the name that Buco had called him or the name of the woman he talked about. The one who bled. She tried a number of other keywords until she found some stories she thought might be him. There was little information.

She strangely found the idea that he was a murderer more acceptable than the idea that he had sexually assaulted and murdered a woman. She was horrified by that accusation. Thinking of that night, how he was with her, she just could not believe it to be true. He couldn't be a rapist. She remembered when Buco had a gun pointed at her head, Jack had all but confessed to the offense; but really, given the circumstances, that made sense to her. It wasn't exactly the best time to say, "I didn't do that, but I am still dangerous." Sometimes it was better to let people be wrong.

Trying to remain as objective as possible, she continued to consider the possibility. As she debated the options of how evil he might be, she was replaying in her mind what the detectives had shared. When they spoke with her, they made the distinction between "responsible for" and "wanted for questioning in." Those were different statements, that Jack was "responsible" for these deaths, and "wanted in questioning" for this other crime. She took solace in that fact. No, he was not a rapist. A hired gun? Yes. She did not doubt that for a minute.

Once she returned to her life, people were calling her constantly, wanting her story, wanting pictures of her and Charles, wanting interviews, anything. There was even an investigative report that had all of the hostages featured, each giving their own perspective. They offered her significant amounts of money, but she declined. They were persistent, so she released a statement thanking everyone for their kindness, but still refused to be featured on television. Although they heard from Charles, who was now in discussion regarding movie rights, Charles did not know her story. What everyone really wanted to know was what happened to the woman behind that door? Rebecca knew society loved stories about the abuse of women. The more horrific, the better. It provided feelings of pity and superiority for some, feelings of arousal for others. She told no one. She would not lie about it again.

She returned to work for a while, but eventually left. She could no longer be effective with the story as national news. Her entire team lost the ability to argue with her, and although that was nice at first, it quickly became evident that they saw her differently. They too wanted to know. She would hear them talking amongst themselves. "What do you think happened?" "Do you think that's all true?" "Has she said anything?" They would linger in her office after meetings, waiting to be the one she would turn to, the one she would unburden herself to, offering to help in any way they could, and if she ever needed to talk about anything. Even Tom came poking around, calling, suddenly interested again, apologizing for not being there. She did not call him back.

She quit and decided that she would agree to assist with a book at a price worthy of a sabbatical as long as she could refuse to sign off on anything inaccurate. And so began the second part of her life, a predictable routine of discussions and writing. It was better this way. A few months had passed, and she was making decent progress, cautiously leaving out as many details about Jack as possible and saying nothing of his final discussion with Buco.

She struggled with adjusting to life after "the GetAway incident." She didn't want to be around anyone, but she didn't want to be alone. She consistently existed at just under rage. During the day, she would alternate between frantically cleaning already clean rooms and sitting for hours on the couch, watching mindless television. She found she was no longer able to watch anything intense; it was too disturbing. At night, she was unable to sleep. She was afraid. She would lie there for hours, trying not to think about Jack and the cabin, but for some reason, unable to think of anything else. Finally she would sleep but then wake up in a panic with the feeling that Matt was there. That he had found her. Then she would remind herself that he was dead. He was not coming for her. He was not coming for anyone. She would be unable to go back to sleep, so she would get out of bed and watch more mindless TV. She bought two guns. They were kept fully loaded, one on each floor of her little townhouse. When she did try and sleep, she kept one on the bed with her. Not overly concerned, she suspected this was the normal aftermath of a traumatic event. True enough. She also knew that much of her emotional state was due to Jack, exhausted for want of him.

She thought about him endlessly. The fear that he might find her and the fear that he might not. What would she do if he did come to her? Would she be all right if he didn't? She already knew she would not call the police. This man saved her life. She would not forget that fact. She was pretty clear about what she would do. She knew herself well. He was dangerous. He was wanted by the law. He had killed people. But if he came for her, she knew she would absolutely let him hold her. Not because she owed him anything, but because she still remembered that night so clearly. In those few brief moments with him, she had felt an intimacy she was not aware existed. She wanted to talk to him, to feel him again. Rebecca wanted to tremble.

For the first few months, she thought she saw him everywhere she went: shopping, in the park, driving to the doctor, going to the police station, everywhere. Her mind would tease her with brief glances that she could have sworn were him, but turned out to be regular people doing regular things. He was, of course, the subject of a nationwide manhunt and most likely staying as far from her as possible. It was a sensational story. Nine dead in one night with a hitman hero is national news. She started to accept she would not see Jack again.

She tried to believe he was in hiding—that he would come if he were not in hiding—but she realized that was not true. It was more likely that their time together was not as significant for him as it was for her; and oh, the agony of that. *Could it be true? I was incidental?* She was shaken by that thought. That she would not know his touch. That he would never again hold her, talk to her; never again run his hand through her hair. *Come on, Rebecca. It was so long ago. He doesn't even remember your name.* It was a painful truth to learn it was not possible to have that night again, her dark man and his terrifying embrace. That those feelings of intensity and affection were merely one-sided. He would not look for her, think of her, come. She went out on a few dates, even had a couple heavy make-out sessions with one of them. She considered having sex with him just to force the thoughts of Jack out of her mind, but she decided against it. She was only fooling herself. The date was a nice enough man, but she felt no real connection with him. It would not be right to bring him into her current drama. Then one day, over a year later, Jack appeared.

He just walked up to her. He walked up to her in the parking lot of the grocery store as she unloaded her cart. His appearance was so normal, she would not have noticed him. He had grown a beard and was wearing a baseball cap, jeans, and a black hoodie. He had a bag slung over one shoulder. She stood next to her trunk where she had been loading the car, frozen at his casual approach.

"Hi."

She dropped the grocery bag she was holding, and it fell to the ground, spilling cans and fruit along the parking lot. As it landed, she was already clinging to his neck, tears in her eyes and whispering thank you. His hand slid into her hair, somewhat surprised as he received her greeting.

"Can we get off the street?" he asked.

"Yes." As they drove the two minutes home, she was biting her lip so as not to ask him anything. *Where have you been? Did you really kill everyone? Is what they told me true?*

She pulled into the garage. Leaving him in the family room, she went to the kitchen, quickly throwing the entire bag into the refrigerator.

"You want something to drink?" she offered.

Jack Shelley had somehow ended up in her family room. He was studying a long-dead rose that had been placed on the mantel of the fireplace, petals a delicate brown that would disintegrate upon the slightest disturbance.

"No. Are we alone?"

"Yes."

"Are you expecting anyone?"

"No." She was whispering now. He came closer, looking down at her.

"The fool?"

"No one."

He dropped his bag and took off his cap and tossed it on the chair. He removed his gun and placed it next to the rose.

"Are you all right?"

"Yes." She was still whispering. "Are you?"

"I've been somewhat restricted."

"It was on the news."

"I heard . . . what you did." *He looks so intense. Did not remember him being so intense.* She looked away and shrugged, feeling uncomfortable.

"I interrupted him."

"Yes, you did."

His eyes drifted down to her hair, which now hung at her shoulders. Considerably longer than the last time they were together.

"Your hair," he said thickly. "It's nice." It was such a simple thing to comment on her hair; somehow it sounded so predatory.

"It's grown out a bit," she stammered. Her breathing was starting to shallow. *Was he always this severe?*

Rebecca stepped closer to him. She cautiously brushed his beard. It was thick and dark brown, trimmed close to his face, coarse on her hand. He was silent, looking down at her.

"I was afraid I would never see you again," she whispered.

"Afraid," he repeated.

She nodded.

He reached for her, hand pausing in the air before his fingers grazed the now chestnut strands. They trailed lightly along her neck and then across where she was bitten. She enjoyed the warmth they left behind.

"I wasn't sure I should come." His hand dropped back down to his side. "I've been haunted."

"Haunted?" she whispered. She felt like she might cry, felt like running out the front door, looking away, anything. She had to force herself to stay where she was, to look him in the eye. *Haunted. He said haunted. This isn't just a visit, Rebecca.* She was beginning to understand her longing failed to completely recognize what he was. His voice, his scent, his hands . . . *him.*

In front of her was a ruthless assassin; *and he wanted her.*

He stepped closer. No smile, no playfulness, closer and with purpose.

"I want to know you," he growled.

She nodded. She did not trust her voice. She had no words to give him anyway. She was becoming afraid.

He placed one hand on her waist and said, "Tell me."

"Yes, Jack."

"My God, woman," he said as he shook his head. "How I dreamed of you." Spoken through clenched teeth, it sounded menacing. He leaned down and kissed her, fiercely, sliding his hands along her back, her shoulders, her neck.

When he pulled off his shirt, she noted every scar on his chiseled frame as a victim. Images flashed in her mind of the people he had killed, the blood, the screwdriver, his laugh. *She was a bit of a fighter.* His hands moved so softly and somehow so intently across her body, pulling those images from her mind. He smelled so good; he *felt* so good.

When he took her upstairs, she was still kissing him back, but she was shaking. He removed her shirt, her bra, his hands exploring her body. He slid her jeans down, kneeling in front of her and gently freeing each foot. When he brushed his beard against her thigh, she jumped and cried out. He stood, eyes searching hers; he stopped and dropped his hands to his side.

"You are afraid."

"Yes," she said as a tear slid down her cheek.

"Rebecca, I will do anything you want," he whispered.

"Please don't stop."

His hand moved to wipe the tear from her cheek. He kissed each wrist and placed them on his chest. He held her. He turned down the covers on the bed and gently laid her down. Keeping the rest of his clothes on, he stretched out next to her. She turned to face him, and he rested his forehead against hers. He kissed her sweetly on the mouth and neck, stroking her hair, touching her softly until she stopped shaking, until she reached for him.

Chapter 18

Long after the dog, and the morning before he would first meet Rebecca, William set his bag in the corner of his empty one-bedroom apartment. He was preparing to leave the next day to start the drive out to the GetAway Resort. His place was small, efficient, and clean. There was only the slightest evidence that anyone lived there at all. He had a couch, a lamp, a TV, a twin bed, a radio, and a number of books piled on a small shelf near his bed. It was not all that different from his first apartment, with the addition of a kitchen. He was accustomed to living modestly. Being raised in a crowded boys' home had made him appreciate solitude far more than any possession.

He stepped over the book on the floor and went to refill his coffee. He stepped over the book again to retrieve the paper from outside his door; then he stepped over the book one more time and sat down on the couch. As he settled on the couch, he felt the burn against his back from the woman he had met the night before. She was an angry lover.

He looked at the book on the floor. He honestly couldn't remember how it had come to be in his home. Father Daniels' favorite book. Every few years or so, he would pick it up again. His most recent attempt at reading it was about six months ago. He managed to get through the beginning before he hurled it across the room in an exceedingly rare flash of anger. There it remained. Deliberately incidental. Now he stepped over it as he might any other item in the room.

Last night he couldn't sleep, again. He had walked to the bar down the street. William preferred being alone, but sometimes he wanted to be alone around people. Sitting in the back, observing the Friday night crowd, he noticed her moving around the bar with a couple other young ladies. Probably just old enough to be in this place. They were being loud, not offensive— that female version of loud that is considered fun and bar appropriate. She wore only black: skin-tight black pants with a black leather jacket. Laced boots that went up to her knees. Her hair was the same blue-black of the lines around her eyes. *Fierce* is what came to mind. Her counterparts were sweeter looking, more playful, as they chatted with the men more than willing to buy them drinks. Her darkly painted lips never parted to smile. She sat in silence, glancing at her watch as the others flirted away. He could feel her anger from where he sat. He watched her until he kept looking at her long enough for her to notice. She caught his gaze and glared back at him. He didn't look away. She stood with her drink and approached, sliding into the open chair next to him.

"You want to buy me a drink?" she said in a hostile tone.

"Do you want a drink?"

"Not really."

"All right."

"Do you want to take me home?" she asked while still glaring at him. He finished his drink and stood up. She grabbed his hand and led him out of the bar, briskly walking down the street. The only sound was the clunk her heavy boots made as she walked. She dragged him up the three flights of stairs leading to her apartment. Once inside, she shut the door and attacked him, kissing him violently and clutching the back of his head. She tugged at his shirt, and he pushed her back.

"You're an angry one," he growled.

"Yeah? What, you don't like that?" she asked. She put a condom in his hand and came at him again.

"I don't know; I haven't fucked you yet." He glanced around the room. It was a small place, lived in, clothes and shoes thrown around. It was clear a man lived there.

"Why do you think I brought you here?" she spat back at him. She took off her jacket and tossed it on the floor, revealing a low-cut black shirt. Her slender left arm had at least a dozen slash marks at different stages of healing.

"You want him to walk in on you," he said. She slid up against him, biting the side of his neck.

"I hope so," she replied. She pulled at his shirt again, roughly sliding her hands along his back. "Do you want me to pretend it's something else?" she sneered. He tightly gripped her hair, pulling her back and putting her against the door, making her look at him. She barely glanced up and started tugging at his belt.

"I want you to be present," he said.

"I want you to do whatever you want to me."

"All right."

"I mean it," she insisted.

"Self-destructive revenge?" he asked. He pulled down on her hair harder and kissed her neck.

"Anything. I don't care how much it hurts."

"Like those marks on your arms?" He slid his hand down between her breasts, nuzzling into her neck, running his hands along her body.

"Asshole," she said as she pushed lightly on his chest, her tone full of hate. "What, did I pick the only guy in the bar with a fucking moral compass?"

"If you're mad at him, why do you hurt yourself?"

"Fuck you!" she yelled at him and pushed him away, hard. "Get the fuck off me!" She slapped him. "Asshole." He stepped back and gave her smile.

"You can do better than that."

She stared at him for a second, surprised; she pulled back and clocked him in the face. He smiled again. She pulled back her arm to hit him a second time, and he grabbed her shoulders and pushed her against the door. She gasped and looked at him.

"There you are," he growled down at her as he drew closer. "I have no fucking moral compass, little girl." He let her go, and after a few seconds, she came at him again, still angry, but not hateful.

When she tried to put her mouth on him, he ripped her up by her hair, threw her back on the bed, and stripped off her clothes. When she screamed, he covered her mouth, told her to shut up, and began to violate her with his hand, feeling her muffled cries in his palm until he entered her. When he entered her, he let her scream. He choked her until she was sufficiently afraid, and when he released her, she grabbed his hand and put it back on her throat. At one point she clawed him so badly he turned her over. He bit her, hurt her, sodomized her. He punished her for a while.

They didn't get interrupted. That was good because she turned out to be pretty hot when she stopped trying to hurt him. As they lay there panting, she reached over and put her hand on his chest and moaned appreciatively. When he was getting dressed, she had even pulled on a T-shirt to smoke, appearing quite comfortable, at the moment too self-involved to feel anything else. She pulled forward the collar of her shirt and examined her chest. Then she looked at her legs.

"You didn't leave a mark on me," she said, still smoking and sounding quietly surprised. She could not see him smile as he sat on the edge on the bed, putting on his shoes. He stood up and put his jacket on. He crossed over to where she was and sat down next to her. She flinched when he reached for her. He looked at her, gently pulled up her shirt, and softly kissed her breast.

"Whoa there, cowboy. I can't do that again right now." Then she hissed as she felt his mouth painfully marking her. He slid down her body, kissed her intimately, and did the same to her upper thigh.

"Neither can I," he said. He managed to leave before she became afraid.

On the way down the stairs, he passed a kid. Black and green hair, tattoos up and down both arms. Funny she didn't have any. As he walked by, he spoke to the kid.

"You're late."

The kid paused briefly, confused. William kept walking. Just another interesting few hours.

Flipping open the paper, he scanned the personal ads.

"My dear poet, your services are required to comfort a dying man. Please come today at 10 a.m." It was followed by an address. No phone number.

More poetic than usual. Strange. It was typically just an address or number. He glanced at his watch, considering the ad, the distance. He armed himself, stepped over the book on the floor, and left.

Chapter 19

A S SHE CURLED up in his arms, Rebecca was determined not to sleep for fear he would not be there when she awoke. He slept with his hand resting lightly on her throat. After a while, she had to get up to retrieve the sheets and blankets, which he had thrown on the floor. As she was climbing as softly as she could back into bed, he stirred and opened his eyes. He pulled the covers over them both, kissed her on the head, and went back to sleep.

As hard as she tried, she lost the battle and fell asleep. She slept until morning. When she awoke, Rebecca sat up in bed. He was gone. She threw on a T-shirt and ran downstairs to see the light on in the family room. Relief washed over her, seeing him there. He was on the floor in sweatpants and a T-shirt, doing sit-ups. He stopped when he saw her. He was breathing heavily and sweat covered his face and neck.

"I didn't mean to wake you," he said.

"You didn't. Well, maybe you did. I don't know. I thought you were leaving." She continued down the stairs now, wide awake and planning to make coffee. She paused and said, "Don't just leave, Jack. I mean, please say something, all right?"

He was still seated on the floor. He ran his forehead across his shoulder, wiping away the sweat.

"All right," he said. "Can I take a shower?"

"Sure. Go ahead." She relaxed and went into the kitchen. She stood there a while, staring at the coffeemaker, scoop in hand. *There is a killer in my shower. Does he drink coffee?* She was trapped in this strange absurdity when she realized she was not wearing anything but a T-shirt. She made the coffee and retrieved a pair of sweatpants from the laundry room. She threw them on and stepped outside to have a cigarette.

The yard of her little townhouse was secluded. It was one of the reasons she had wanted the place. She liked privacy. It was still early, and with fall coming, it was brisk outside. A shower sounded good. She was really sore. He had been gentle with her, but it had been so long that her body ached, and let's face it, everything about Jack was big. She smiled. So very gentle. Given her initial fear, she was surprised. She half expected to let him do what he wanted and feel little more than afraid. It didn't matter. She wanted him anyway. As it turned out, she was mistaken. He had been an intensely passionate lover, sweet and attentive. He held her in a way she did not know was possible. She smiled again. Well worth the wait.

She tossed the cigarette into the flower pot that remained there specifically for that purpose and went back inside. When she walked into the kitchen he was standing by the counter. He was shirtless now, hair still wet from the shower; he leaned against the counter, watching her. Seeing him, she was caught by the scars on his chest, much more visible in the light of the kitchen. The one from his forehead did run all the way down his chest, only skipping part of his throat. It was barely visible behind the beard, a small white line. It became much more severe as it moved closer to his heart. She also saw a few large scars, circles and gashes, scattered across his body. She realized she was staring.

"Do you do coffee?" she asked.

"Yes. Thank you."

"Breakfast?"

"Yes. Thank you," he answered.

She started pulling eggs and bacon out of the fridge and fixed their coffee, chatting nervously about nothing. He put on a T-shirt and sat at the table, silently watching her, smiling occasionally. They ate and talked about the day, the weather, trivial matters. She did, anyway. Rebecca was just trying not to ask him, "How long can you stay?"

After breakfast, she showered as quickly as possible and returned to the kitchen in jeans, a T-shirt, and a hint of makeup. Jack was still seated at the table, same cup of coffee in front of him. She poured herself another cup and sat with him.

"Want some more?" she asked.

He put his hand on her arm, leaned over, and kissed her slowly and softly, and with intent. Frightening and exhilarating; already starting to tremble, she kissed him back. He gently took her back upstairs and made love to her again.

Afterward, he was leaving little kisses along her

shoulders. She was clinging to him, a few tears still escaping, along with a few soft giggles. She felt him smile against her neck before he rolled onto his back, leaving his hand on her stomach.

They were quietly happy for a while.

"Are you expecting anyone today?" he asked.

"No," Rebecca said. "I'm rarely expecting anyone, Jack. Don't worry."

"Do you have a man?"

"Well, I would hope not." She laughed. "You don't care, do you?"

"Not at the moment." He smiled, his hand running softly along her body.

"No, Jack," she offered. "No men." *Not since you.* She laughed again. "Why, do you have a girl? Because I do care."

"No."

He rolled over and ran his fingers softly across her cheek. He was not smiling anymore. "I'd like to stay here for a little while. Would that be all right with you?" he asked.

"Yes." She tried not to answer too quickly.

"Rebecca."

"Yes."

"The police are looking for me."

"I know."

"If they come, I want you to tell them I forced my way in here. You had no choice. You were in fear for your life. All right?"

"I don't want to do that," she said quietly.

"I know."

"They wouldn't believe me anyway," she said after considering his suggestion. "People know we were together."

"They will believe me," he said simply and returned to lying on his back.

"People saw us together at the cabin, Jack."

"I'll tell them that's where you got away from me."

He looked over at her and raised his arm up, inviting her closer. She slid toward him and put her head on his chest. He wrapped his arm around her.

"They won't believe that," she was whispering now, "that you hunted me down after all this time."

"I did."

Rebecca melted into him. She did not completely trust her voice, so she nodded. She swallowed and cleared her throat.

"You can stay as long as you want."

Chapter 20

WHEN WILLIAM ARRIVED at the address listed in the personal ad, he parked and looked around. He was in what appeared to be a middle-class neighborhood. There were children riding bikes down the street, a couple of dogs running around; it seemed peaceful enough. He walked up to the door and knocked. A nun opened up the door. He stood, thinking he may be at the wrong address, until she opened the door wider and stood aside for him to enter. She could have been about forty years old, pale and thin, with a small wisp of brown hair slipping out from beneath her habit. She did not smile at him, and she did not speak. She turned and walked down the hall. He slid his hand inside his jacket and followed. At the end of the hall, she opened another door and gestured for him to enter. He did not move.

"Father is asking for you," she said with a reverence that indicated she expected all people to be as obedient to Father's wishes as she was. William eyed her suspiciously, and then entered the room. She followed. In front of him sat an old priest, with white hair on his head and a long white beard. He was seated in a large green chair with the Bible open on his lap. The priest sat up when they entered and smiled. It took William a minute to recognize that it was Father Daniel sitting in front of him. He was much older, weathered, and a bit disheveled. Gone was the bright red hair and beard, but his eyes were as clear as William remembered.

"My boy!" the priest announced, slowly rising from his chair. He crossed the room to where William stood frozen. "Oh, my boy!" he said again as he embraced him.

"Come in! Come in! Sit with me! I have been looking for you these past few months." He put his arm around William's back and ushered him to a chair across from him. "You are found!" he said as they sat. "Please, Sister, bring us a drink. William?"

"Uh . . ." He could barely speak.

"How about tea? Yes, some tea for us, please." The sister quietly left the room.

The old priest sat smiling, just looking at him.

"How long has it been, my boy? Twenty years? How very long!"

"Yes."

"Still, here you are. Come to see an old man now. It is good to see you. My, you are a grown man. It is always a surprise to see one of my boys all grown up." The sister returned with a small cart piled with biscuits, cookies, cream, sugar, and tea. She rolled it to the father, prepared his tea, and coughed at William for direction.

"Black is fine, thank you." William was pulling himself together. He felt a bit of anger at this ambush—anger and a hollow, deep ache at the suddenness of seeing the priest again. The sister handed him his tea and stepped back. He held it in front of him like a shield.

"Thank you, Sister. You may leave us now. We have much to talk about," the father said. William shifted in his seat, and she departed. "The sisters care for me now," Father Daniel offered. "Did you know Father Stephen has passed?"

"I heard."

"I was there at the end, William. Last rites." The priest paused thoughtfully. "After that, he did not suffer," he said. "I did not see you at the service?"

William did not respond.

"I imagine you want to know why I have looked for you, eh? Well, I suppose I should tell you that I am likely dying, boy. That's what they tell me, anyway. So, when a man learns he is dying, he starts thinking of his past, his life; has he done all he had set out to do? That sort of thing. Seeing Father Stephen again, I remembered my time at Saint Ignatius. I became nostalgic. I started thinking about you and how much time we spent together at the ring. Us and that dog, eh? I wrote you when I left, but it was too late. You were already lost. Anyway, I wanted to see how you were doing." He sipped his tea. "So, I followed a suggestion from Father Stephen and here you are. You see, when a man is dying, he gets whatever he wants. Why, just look at this tray! I ask for tea, and we have this. A dying man can do anything. He gets to demand things, gets to be surly, gets to be wise. Everyone just says, 'Well, he is dying, after all. Let's give him more cookies.' I can force people to come sit with me, to talk with me long after they are uncomfortable. I see them there, desperate to leave, emotionally exhausted at trying to remain available for the dying priest. They patiently wait to be dismissed." He smiled. "Yes, a dying man can have anything . . . except, of course, what he really wants. Still, as God wills."

William said nothing. He was trying to digest what Father Daniel was saying. He only looked at the priest with slight confusion.

"Strange way for people to find you, William, but then I don't really use the phone either. It's mainly doctors that call here now anyway. So, the sisters care for me," he said again. "They are good to me," he went on. "It is good to have women around. They drag men from our savagery. They civilize us. They are stronger than us in many ways, you know. It takes strength to care for the pitiful, to clothe them and feed them; strength to put your needs second, to return hate with love." He sipped his tea and reached for a biscuit. "Tell me, William, did you marry?"

"No."

"Children?"

"No."

"Ah! Are you considering the priesthood?"

"No." He swallowed hard.

"Well, my boy, then you should marry! Who will keep you civilized? You have the love of a woman though, yes?"

"No."

"Ah, nor have I." He smiled gently. "I always thought that would be quite something, to be held that way. To be loved by such a gentle creature as God has made. Really loved, William. Not like that nonsense that went on with Father Stephen. I mean a goodly woman."

William did not respond.

"But now to look at you! You look well! You have on nice clothes, nice shoes! You must be doing something of worth. What do you do, my boy?"

"I am an independent contractor."

"What is that?"

"In risk management. I . . . decrease risk."

"Hmm. Decrease risk, eh? It must be profitable! It is good to see you doing so well, but what is that on your face, William?"

"It's . . . a scar." He was starting to feel as if he might vomit.

"Yes." The priest leaned forward in his chair and locked eyes with the assassin. "I wonder. Did it cause you much pain?"

Silence.

"No more than any other," William said with a thickness in his voice.

"Yes. I imagine that is true," Father Daniel said. "How deep does it go, boy?" he asked, still leaning forward. William did not respond. He swallowed hard and looked down at his tea. His leg was shaking. He was having a hard time catching his breath.

Silence.

"I hear you've become quite the poet?"

William paled. He drew in a sharp breath. All the blood seemed to drain from his body. Tears invading, he could not look up; he could barely speak.

"Father . . . please."

"Please? What, is this not true?" The priest sounded innocent, but William could feel Father Daniel looking at him. The silence dragged on until he was forced to respond.

"I have heard that too," he struggled.

"Do not mock me, boy. Speak."

"Yes," he whispered.

"Why? Why did you choose this?"

"I . . . it just kind of happened." He shook his head. "I . . ."

Silence came again.

"So tell me then, what is the cost for one of your poems?" The priest spoke gently, continuing his agonizing inquiry. William was trapped. He could not move. He could not look up. He could do nothing. He was again a young boy, held captive by this priest.

"It depends," he said as a couple of tears slid from his eye.

"It depends. I see. Is the cost greater for the more pitiful? Is it greater for a woman?" William took a couple of deep breaths and set his tea back down on the tray. His hand went to his forehead.

"I don't know." His answer was honest. It had never come up. He learned a long time ago that men liked to kill their own women.

"I see," the priest said softly. "What about a child?" He rose and moved to the seat next to William. "Well, what if I need your services? How would I know, boy?"

"You?" William swallowed thickly, and his voice was starting to shake.

The father placed his hand firmly on William's

forearm. The assassin was repulsed by the feel of it, the weight of it sitting there, unwavering. Then came rage. A dark rage like he had never known began to claw its way through him with sharp and painful waves, demanding release, demanding to be heard. He even thought vaguely of shooting the father. This damn priest who had sought him out, who invited him to his home, apparently just to invade, expose, and shove his face in the light. Images flashed through his mind of blood, hate, and darkness. He would not have become this trembling, crying waif now caged by this old man if he were back in the dark. If he were away from this sadistic priest and his forced confession. He glared at the father with a terrible sneer.

"Well, for you, Father, it would be less. I would give *you* a discount. A bargain, really." He laughed harshly. His hate burned into the man. His tears now dry, he met the priest's eyes with his own and smiled, daring him to continue. "Is it one of the sisters? Hell, I'll do it for free." The priest was unmoved. He received this hate with his gentle hand remaining heavy on the assassin's arm.

"And why not?" Father Daniel asked. "I have the same hatred in my heart, the same rage, the same desires. The Holy Father says violence committed in your heart is the same as the deed." He squeezed William's arm. "We are all the same vile creatures, William, but you are wrong. There would be great cost," he said softly. "Great cost for us both."

William looked away and said, "We are not the same."

"Oh yes, my boy, we are! We only make different choices. I choose the grace of God. I choose redemption." The priest smiled. "Only God can judge man; it is not for an old priest to do that." He continued, as if William were no longer there, "I wonder if it brings comfort or pain knowing that you have a choice? Knowing you can choose to be gentle, that you can choose love and light, you can choose to accept redemption? Eh, either way, that is not my doing. That is not my fight. Only God can change the heart, lad, and that is between you and Him. I have no power over that." The priest patted his arm. "My boy, I can see how weary you are. You are now dismissed. Please come and visit me again soon. I am dying, you know; did I mention that?"

"You want me to come back?" William spat at him, horrified.

The priest smiled. "Of course! I love you, my boy. I have missed you! It has been too long." The father stood, and William followed. The old man embraced him again, smiling. "Soon. But next time, you will stay for dinner. You are a man now; you need real food, eh? Not tea." It was more of an instruction than an invitation.

"All right," he stammered, uncertain if he was lying, but agreeing, as he could not remain any longer in this brightly lit nightmare.

William left. He walked slowly out of the room, out of the house; by the time he reached the car, he was running. He dove into the car and pulled away. When he was a safe distance from the house, he pulled over and shut off the car. His hands were trembling. He closed his eyes and remained there for a while. Eventually, he started the car and pulled out in the direction of the expressway.

Such was the fragile state of the assassin when he pulled into the GetAway Resort after an exceedingly long five-hour drive. Such was his state when he met the woman who spoke of the choices of the unsick and told him everyone can be helped. The woman who touched his cheek, who cared for the pitiful.

He had left GetAway at a brisk jog. He kept moving for at least an hour before he came across a car. One wonderful car parked alone in the dark of a lone country bar closed for the night. Someone too drunk to drive. He borrowed the car. He made only one stop at a storage locker to pick up the go bag he had stashed there, complete with ID, clothes, and money. After securing his belongings and perhaps having nowhere else to go, William returned to the priest. He left the car at least five miles away from the little cottage. When he arrived, the sun was just starting to rise.

The good father opened the door wearing an old maroon robe. His hair was a wild white mess on top of his head, and he was yawning. He had obviously been asleep, groggy and surprised to find William at the door.

"William? Come in." William entered in silence. Father Daniel inspected him. He was covered head to toe in black and copper smears, mud, and sweat. The priest gave no visible response. He simply waved at William to follow and yawned, turning toward the kitchen. William paused at the door, knowing he was filthy. He took off his shoes and followed. He heard the father speaking in the other room and froze until he figured out he was on the phone. William approached the kitchen and overheard the father saying he had a guest that would look after him and there was no need for them to come today.

"I warn you, my boy, I have not made coffee in many

years." William remained in the doorway to the kitchen as the father crossed over to the counter. The old man flipped on the small television in the corner more out of daily habit than anything else. The response was immediate.

"Nine dead and several others wounded" flashed across the bottom of the screen, and the program had a reporter who was informing viewers of the same.

"Father, I . . ." William began, but Father Daniel held up his hand, silencing him, and remained focused on the television. William obeyed, remaining silent and looking down at the ground. After a few minutes, the priest came forward and stood in front of him. William could feel the priest looking at him, judging him, seeing the evidence of death smeared in filth across his clothes. William kept looking at the floor. The priest embraced him.

"My boy, are you all right?"

"Yes, Father." William swallowed. He had never known the father to approach with anything other than love, and yet he still found it painfully surprising.

The priest reached for the television to turn it off as the reporter announced new information from the victims related to the assassination of a man in police custody, an unidentified hero, and a woman who risked her life to save a young girl.

"Wait," William said, intently watching the program. He was now visibly shaken.

"Put down your bag and sit. I will make breakfast," Father Daniel said. He set coffee and water on the table.

"I am not hungry," William replied and sat.

"I will make breakfast for me."

The priest prepared food to the best of his ability while they listened to the news. They reported that the victims were all in stable condition and being treated at the local hospital for injuries sustained during the attacks. They kept repeating the same handful of facts until the father brought two plates of food to the table and sat down. He turned off the television to eat. He did not inquire.

William accepted the coffee and slowly began to speak. He told Father Daniel everything that happened at the cabin. He relayed every single thought and every single act of the night before. He held nothing back. The father, now unable to finish his breakfast, listened quietly. When William again grew silent, the old man sighed.

"Such a tale, my boy. Give me a minute to consider," he said softly. "I am thankful you are not hurt, but William, so many men."

"I reacted poorly."

"The news is calling you a hero."

"The news is incorrect."

"You regret this, then? You regret what you have done?" Father Daniel asked.

"I think I regret I did not leave when I had the opportunity."

The priest breathed deeply, accepting these statements with some difficulty. He was unaccustomed to the dark honesty in William's response. After a few breaths, he pressed on.

"I notice you did not leave," Father Daniel said. "Rather the opposite. Why would that be?"

"I wasn't myself last night, priest," William sneered with a hint of anger and began picking at his plate of cold eggs.

"Even still, hesitating to kill someone seems the right course of action."

"That has never concerned me, Father," William said as his voice grew quieter, realizing he was again trapped in confession.

"Murder does not concern you, but I believe you are concerned for this woman. The way you spoke of her. Your reaction to the news. Why do you think that is?"

"I don't know. Ever take a bone from a dog?"

"Perhaps so, my boy. Perhaps so, but you are a grown man. I am certain you have known an unfinished kiss. What is different now?"

"I enjoyed her company."

"Her company?"

"Enjoyed talking to her."

"Speak, boy. I am still a man."

"She was . . ."

"You wanted her," Father Daniel offered.

"No." William halted. "Yes, very much."

"As you said, she was a beautiful woman." The priest shrugged.

"That is not it."

"Tell me what you think," the priest said evenly.

"The soul gropes in search of a soul," William said softly.

"How's that?"

"I don't fit, Father," William paused and sighed, looking down at his plate. "I have never fit, but with this woman, for a moment, I felt I did. Talking to her, being with her was . . . yes, when she beckoned me, kissed me, yes, I wanted her. More than anything."

"Yes, William. I understand," Father Daniel said gently.

"Of course, I realize she feared I would kill her."

"Kill her?"

"She was afraid of me. Kissing me as she did; I assumed it to be an attempt to save her life."

"That did not stop you?"

"I wanted her."

"She was afraid of you."

"I found it unlikely to have her any other way."

"Oh, William, no," Father Daniel groaned.

"I did not want to force her, Father. I thought I might change her mind temporarily. I was interrupted, and I was not expecting these men."

"I see."

"This woman, she lied to them about me. I heard her." William shook his head. "That makes sense. It's strategic, right?"

"I suppose, yes," Father Daniel agreed.

"She gave her shirt to that girl."

"It sounds as if she offered more than that," the priest reminded.

"That was . . . a mistake," William said quietly.

"No, boy. I do not think so."

"You did not see her, Father. It was a mistake."

"We disagree." The priest waved his hand.

"Father . . . she . . ." William struggled, trying to explain. "I am no longer certain she was acting out of fear." William stopped speaking and sat back in his chair.

Father Daniel saw he was suddenly exhausted. He patted William on the hand as he stood.

"The poet has lost his words," the priest remarked.

"Yeah." Too tired to be irritated, William relented.

Father Daniel walked to his room and pulled the covers down on his bed. He then pointed toward the shower.

"Come, my boy. You will clean up and sleep. You are safe here. We will talk more when you wake up, eh?" William followed the priest and eventually slept.

Several hours later, he awoke to find the father was gone. It took him about an hour before he figured out where the old man went. He had taken it upon himself to go visit Rebecca in the hospital. He returned the next morning to William pacing in the office.

"She is well. She is well," the priest offered as he walked in, weary from the drive.

"You saw her?"

"I am a priest. I go wherever I want."

"You didn't tell me, Father."

"I had my own agenda, boy. I did not want to go for yours," Father Daniel said, sitting down.

"She is all right?"

"She is well. We prayed together. My boy, she is a beautiful soul. You should do well to marry such a woman."

"A beautiful soul," William repeated. "She would do well to refuse me."

"Hmm? I seem to remember you spoke differently before. What was it you said? Something about her voice? The burn of her dangerous hand? Ah, it was so lovely. I suppose I have forgotten. I am old. Well, it is settled then. She is a beautiful woman with a beautiful soul. She will find another man." He raised an eyebrow at William. "You may thank me, though. I brought her a rose for you."

"Thank you, Father."

Although he was welcomed in by the old priest, it was less so by the sisters. They were not happy with this selfish man who seemed to not want to leave the father's side. Always there, always pestering him, not letting him rest. They were like children, the two of them. This boy kept the father up all hours of the night, taking into no account the fact that Father Daniel was in poor health. Still, he was dying, after all, and seemed to find joy in this man; and so they tolerated his presence.

William remained there until the father's quiet death. Father Daniel remained relentless. It seems invasive to reveal the intimate nature of the discussions that occurred between the assassin and the priest. They were at the very least philosophical. Suffice it to say, the boy began to understand, and the priest was granted witness.

Chapter 21

J ACK DID STAY with Rebecca. He stayed and stayed and kept staying. They did nothing. They would talk, curl up on the couch and watch television, eat, make love, and repeat. They went to pick up his car, but after that, he rarely left the house. She only left out of necessity. They spent the first few days catching up. Well, she did. She told him everything that had happened since her return from the cabin: leaving work, talking to the police, the book. The origins of her new life. Jack still reflected whatever she said. He did not offer any information.

He asked her about her family, her childhood, where she grew up; he asked her everything. Past relationships, past sins, religious ideals: everything. It was conflicting for Rebecca. She had always found it draining to talk about herself, but she couldn't help but be humbled by his interest. Also, it was difficult not to ask him anything substantial in return. She thought perhaps that might change with time, but for then he remained a mystery. She was happy to accept his silence provided he kept looking at her the way he did.

She struggled to adapt to this new environment. She had never lived with anyone before, and had certainly not expected to be making meals for a killer. At first, he was still intense, still frightening. Trembling under him continued to be a nightly rapture. He remained the steady and quiet observer, gentle and warm. Rebecca began to transition from feelings of intensity and nervousness to feelings of comfortable silence. They both had their own specific glory.

They started to spend their days in domestic solitude: groceries, bills, and other mundane adventures. He ordered the newspaper and spent his mornings with it at the table. He had been there about two months when she first watched him take out the trash. She was in the kitchen looking at the most recent draft of the book and heard him behind her. She was momentarily confused. *There is a domesticated killer in my house.*

It was three months before she heard him really laugh. He was seated on the couch watching television. She was writing out some Christmas cards, and it actually scared her. She peeked in the family room and saw a hint of what he might have been, sitting with his feet up on the coffee table, appearing relaxed and laughing at the TV. She smiled.

It was wonderful at first. After a couple weeks, she was nervous. After a few months, she was beside herself. She kept expecting him to leave. And even though she had made it quite clear he could stay as long as he wanted, she wanted—she *needed*—to know how long that would be. His quiet and constant attention left her feeling so deeply loved. Talking to him, seeing him smile, sleeping next to him. Her lovely Jack. His arms were the safest place in the world. When he spoke, it was thoughtful and honest. When he listened, it was intently and completely. Those days of peaceful affection were unlike anything she had ever known, and she was saddened at the knowledge they would soon end. Other than his warmth, he left no evidence that he was even there. Nothing was out of place or dirty or even touched. His small pile of belongings was the only evidence of his existence: that and the money that kept showing up in her account unannounced. She had fought over the phone with the bank for thirty minutes before she realized it was from him.

Despite knowing he was only a temporary addition to her life, the more she grew to know him, the more she started to love him. The knowledge he might leave any day was agonizing, but she actively hid those feelings from him. At times, it would become unbearable, and she would have to bite her lip so she wouldn't attack him with a barrage of questions, demanding to know how he felt, what he wanted, why he was here. *Is it true? Do you love me or are you just hiding?* When that happened, she tried to remember he was going to leave, not to ruin these moments with female inquisition. Then at night, he would hold her, and she would be all right for a while. He held her as he did everything else: silently, fearlessly, and with the perfect blend of attention and disregard.

At about the six month mark, she awoke to find him gone. There was a note on the counter that said "Back tonight." She immediately began crying. Where would he go? His car was gone. What was he doing? She was crying because she knew there were only a few things he could be doing, and none of them were pleasant. She knew he was getting ready to leave.

She cried on and off for a while, took a shower, cleaned up, and waited for him to come back. He returned in the early evening. He did not offer to say where he had been. She did not ask. He came in and sat on the couch with her before he suggested they go get a drink somewhere. Get out of the house. She was horrified by this unusual behavior.

"Someone might recognize you?" she offered.

"Maybe . . . we'll see. It's been a while. The sketch didn't look that much like me. Eyewitnesses are usually distracted."

"I don't think we should, Jack."

"Well, we have to try sometime. At some point we might want to leave the house together."

"I know, but are you sure?"

"When I am with you, people look at you. If it feels wrong, we can leave."

She dressed to go out, intentionally wearing a snug black dress with a plunging neckline. She tugged at it, trying to cover the remnants of the wound on her chest. It was more provocative than what she usually wore, but she was hopeful to be the center of attention. When she came downstairs, she felt his eyes on her. They drove to a small martini bar. He chose a booth at the back.

Her entrance attracted the look of a man at the bar. He was clean cut, with a regular build and blond hair that had been styled to appear messy. He presented as wealthy and was dressed to support that idea. He was seated next to another similar-looking man, and he leaned over and said something to him. It was evident they had been there a while. Both men glanced at her, and Blondie turned sideways in his seat, facing her. From the bar, they could barely see Jack. She was relieved he did not seem to notice. He seemed quite comfortable.

"You look nice," he said and then nodded toward the bar. "See, it's like I am not even here."

"Thank you," she said, looking only at him. "It's a bit low. I was hoping to be a distraction."

"You are." His tone made her blush. "You stole his breath at the door." She considered his words and smiled.

"You do that sometimes; you sound like a poet."

"I've heard that."

"One of your little girlfriends?"

"A priest."

"A priest?" she repeated. "Really?" She felt the questions starting to come and hesitated. "Well, it's true."

They ordered some wine and settled in. It was strange being in public with him. She had not experienced that before. This was the first time they had actually left the house together. She was nervous. He scanned the menu and asked if she wanted anything. She said no. Rebecca was sitting up completely straight, obviously uncomfortable with this whole situation.

"Strange to be out, isn't it?"

"It is," he said, eyeing her carefully. "Think we will get used to it?"

"I guess so. What do you think?"

"I'm thinking I should take you out more often."

"Yeah, this is actually our first date, isn't it?"

"True. That didn't occur to me. I think you're uncomfortable."

"No. I'm fine. This is nice." She sounded as convincing as she could. He raised his eyebrows at her, surprised at her lie.

"Is it being here with me or your friend at the bar?"

"You," she lied again.

"Well, I think we are old news now."

"At least until the movie comes out," she offered.

"Yes, that's right, the movie. Who do you think will play us?"

"Good question."

"Hmm. Do you think I will be the villain or the hero?"

"I guess we'll see."

"Are you going to see it?" he asked.

"Oh, probably. I would like to know what happened. I only know my side."

Blondie smiled at her, and she quickly looked away. He then leaned over to his friend and said something. They both stared at the table and smiled again. Had she been here in other company, she would have met their gaze, dared them to approach. As it was, she was not in other company. She no longer had this luxury. Jack noticed her response and glanced at their reflections in the mirror behind the bar. He moved to get out of his seat.

"What are you doing?" Rebecca said frantically, grabbing his arm. He stopped. "Don't."

"All right," he said and settled back down.

"He's just drunk. It's not worth it," she continued, as if he had not agreed. "He might want to go outside or something?"

Jack smirked at her. His eyes lit up, and he started to laugh. He kept laughing, really laughing at what she had said. Despite herself, she chuckled with him.

"Well, he might," she offered weakly, still laughing.

"You mean fisticuffs?" He laughed. "Do men still do that?" he said seriously, with the hint of laughter still in his voice.

"Don't they? I don't know. I think so!"

"Well, I guess I would have to go outside then." He raised his eyebrows and shrugged.

"Would you?" She kept her hand on his arm.

"That guy is not going outside," Jack said.

"What would you do?" she asked quietly.

He did not respond at first. He considered the question and then said, "I don't know. I haven't had that type of fight since I was a kid. I can usually talk my way out of it."

"But would you . . . go?"

"Why don't you ask me what you really want to ask me?"

"I just don't want any trouble," she whispered, ignoring his question. "You aren't worried about it, are you? You don't worry about anything."

"I am not worried about that guy."

"When?" She spoke with obvious cynicism. "When do you worry?"

He smiled at her. He asked for a kiss. She slid over closer and kissed him sweetly on the mouth. She was waiting for his next evasion when she realized he probably asked for a kiss to bring her closer. Not to evade her question, but to answer it. He raised his hand and briefly traced his fingers across her throat. He did that often.

"When we were at the cabin, I was worried. I came back and saw what was going on; I was considering what to do. I was watching the lobby."

"You were?"

"Through the window. I saw that man grab you. I saw that room, the blood, the fight." He took her hand. "I still worry. I see that, sometimes, at night. His hand on your throat, that room. Then I get out of bed and check that the doors are all locked."

"You do?"

"Sometimes."

"I didn't know that." Thoughts of that night flooded her mind, remembering the lobby. Realizing he had been watching created a strange feeling. It was not quite shame, but certainly uncomfortable. She was trying to recall exactly what had occurred. What he would have seen. She was aware he saw Matt was dead. She did not consider what the room must have looked like, especially to him. He would have noticed everything.

"Jack, I am okay," she said, and then paused, considering. They had never really talked about it. She squeezed his hand. "He didn't rape me. I don't . . . I mean I hope you remember that. I just don't like to talk about it." She was whispering now, forcing herself to look him in the eye. "He was going to. He could have. It was awful. He touched me. He said horrible things. He hurt me, but it was a long time ago." Jack did not respond. "I was afraid, but I don't think about it anymore. It was a few bad moments. I am not going to let it interfere with me any longer than it already has. I want you to do the same."

"You don't think about it?" He nodded at her chest. "Even when you see that?"

"When you see yours, do you always think about where it came from?" She nodded at the scar on his face.

"Sometimes."

"Is that what you think of when you see mine?"

"Yes." He swallowed. "I am reminded of my inaction."

"You were a little busy saving several other people at the time, as I recall." Jack said nothing, and she continued.

"When I left the hospital, they gave me a cream for it. An ointment, you know . . . directions to change the bandage and all that. Every day, I would peel off the tape and apply that stupid cream. Every day, I would look at it, inspect it, see if it was healing, wonder how bad it would scar. You know what I thought about? I thought about you. I thought about how gentle you were. How you took care of me. How you sounded when you spoke. How your hands felt. You. Not him. Never him," Rebecca said, and added, "I feel like I am ruining our first date. This conversation is becoming too intense."

"No, Rebecca, you are not ruining anything," he said softly. "How about some more wine?"

"I think I've had too much already."

They finished their drinks and rose to leave. When they walked past the bar, Jack never turned his head. He kept his eyes on her. He took her hand when they walked to the car, held it in silence as they drove home. As they entered the house, she turned and headed upstairs to change. He followed and asked her not to. Playfully, she told him her dress might get wrinkled. He assured her that it would. Feeling tipsy and bold, she asked him to repeat what he had said about the man at the bar. "Tell me again how he caught his breath. Stole his breath. Tell me more. Will you keep talking like that? Like a poet?" He did.

He held nothing back.

Chapter 22

IT WAS CLOSE to midnight when she realized he was no longer next to her. Not too unusual—sometimes he couldn't sleep. She rolled over to where he had been, snuggling into his scent and the warmth his body had left behind. As she settled into his pillow, she smiled with disbelief at his words from the night before.

He began playfully enough, talking about her body, her dress. She had smiled when he said she was a nightmare and a dream. *The dangerous glory of you in rapture.*

Slowly, he became more affectionate until he said such painfully beautiful things she felt tears in her eyes. "I exist in wonder of your smile. I hold you in the agony that it may never be again." When he whispered, "You are my light," she placed a trembling hand on his mouth to silence him. She was shaking, and he smiled down at her and remarked she hadn't done that in a while. Before he made love to her he had whispered two final words: "*Anything. Always.*"

He had not said he loved her, but only those two little words. They were so simple and so powerful. They were also frightening. *Anything. Always.* He would not say those things if he didn't care for her. He had many faults, but she knew he was not a liar. She was slightly amazed at his honesty, his boldness, his willingness to speak in such a manner. People didn't usually speak that openly unless they were going off to war or dying or something.

She sat up. She put on her robe and went downstairs to find him seated by the fireplace, looking into the fire. He held a drink in his hand. It was something hard, something she did not usually have around the house. He had a manila envelope in the seat next to him. She came in and sat down on the couch across from him.

"You're leaving, aren't you?" she whispered.

"I'm considering it."

Rebecca felt like she couldn't breathe.

"I've been here for a long time." He was not looking at her. He took a drink and added, "I have to do something. I've been turning down work."

"What? When?"

His voice was steady, but she noticed his hand starting to grip the fabric on the arm of the chair.

"I keep waiting for you to ask me to leave. How long are you going to let me stay here?"

"As long as you want."

"How can you mean that?" He sounded angry. "You ask me nothing. You know what I did. No doubt you have seen the news, talked to the police. Didn't you hear that I hurt people? That I raped a woman? Tortured her to death?"

"I don't believe that," she said. "I mean . . . about that woman." *I know you are a killer.*

"You don't want to believe it," he said. And at that statement, she almost yelled at him. Almost. She managed to clench her teeth together and glared at him instead.

"I do know the difference, Jack. I don't want to believe it, and I don't believe it. I didn't believe it when I heard it."

"No?"

"No."

"Why not?" He was cold, angry, challenging her.

"I just don't. You think I would let you stay here? Let you touch me if I thought you did that?"

"I am certain you would not."

"Is this why you're down here? Sitting in the dark, thinking about leaving?" she snapped at him. She knew she was getting loud. "Because what? I'm naïve? Because I care about you? What? Are you going to tell me that I'm wrong?" She was now furious. Not because of what he said, but because he was down there alone and thinking about leaving. Leaving even after everything he had said to her just a few hours ago.

"Then why don't you just ask me?"

"I'm trying, Jack."

He closed his eyes, took a breath, and then looked at her, still angry.

"You wanted to ask if I would have killed him, right? That guy at the bar? Probably. His friend? Probably. Everyone there? Why not. It doesn't bother me. It never has. I don't know why." He looked again at the fire and added, "That man from the cabin called you a hero, called us heroes," he sneered. "I am no hero."

"You saved my life."

"Do you know why I involved myself with you? Why I spoke to you in the first place? Took a stroll around the lake? I knew that man was too interested in you, and I didn't want the police showing up. I put you on display. Understand? Made it clear you had company. You were a task. I'll admit an intriguing one, an attractive one, but a task. I didn't expect . . ." he trailed off a bit, took a breath, and continued. "I almost left you there anyway."

"But you didn't leave me there," Rebecca whispered.

"You want to know what I thought when I saw that man grab you in the lobby?" He looked at her coldly. "*Mine.*"

Rebecca caught a gasp in her throat before it had a chance to escape. She managed to return his icy glare until he again began to watch the fire.

"So, I decided I'll just go get her. *Get* you. Not help you, not save you. Get you because *I* was not done with you." He glanced at her with terrible eyes and said, "I didn't save those people; they were in my way."

"You don't know my life. Rebecca. You don't even know my *name*. I know why you don't ask. You don't want to know." He took a drink and said, "I kill people for money."

"Jack, you don't have to . . ." she started.

"You need know that. I hurt people. I murder people. A lot of people. Twenty years' worth. So many people, I'm not sure I remember them all. At least I used to. Now I rise in the morning just to hear you say 'Jack.'" Then he added, "I think I might be evil. You need to know that too. You are right. I didn't kill that woman. I didn't rape her, didn't torture her to death; but I know I *could*."

"I have money. I have money that I don't even want. I know you don't care about that, but I can take care of you, give you anything you want. I will *do* anything you want. We can travel, we can do that. We can see the world. We can sit on the couch. I don't care." His eyes moved from the fire to the drink in his hand.

"With you I feel . . . *I feel.* It's like some glorious torture. My God, I don't want to go back to that life."

He let go of the chair and painfully opened his hand, realizing what he had been doing.

"I know it is wrong to ask you to have . . . a retired . . . I'm not even sure I can make this real, but if you would have me, I want to stay with you. I love you completely."

He reached into the envelope next to him, pulled out a small black box, and held it up feebly. In this box there were two rings.

She started crying, stunned. She had fully assumed this would be his departure. Of course she knew what he was. She had tried so hard to not acknowledge that part of his life that she was unprepared for his confession. Rebecca had always assumed he would leave before she forced this conversation, or as a result of her attempt. She certainly was not expecting his surprising words of love and a little black box.

Looking at him sitting there, he seemed so broken. She desperately wanted to go to him, to hold him and let him bury his face into her chest. To stroke his hair and tell him it did not matter. *I love you. I don't care what you did. I don't care what you were. I love you.* Instead she forced herself to stay on the couch.

"Well, I've always wanted to see Italy," she said softly.

He didn't move at first. It was as if he didn't hear her. He very slightly turned his head, still not looking at her.

"Yeah?" he said with a thickness in his voice. He moved from the chair to his knees on the floor in front of her. He put his hands on either side of her legs, one holding the box and one holding the envelope. He finally looked up at her and saw she was crying.

"I didn't mean to make you cry."

"Give me that ring," she said as she took it from his hand.

He put his head down on her lap. She held him and stroked his hair. After a while, she took the envelope from his other hand. She reached inside and pulled out handful of some type of financial documents.

"What is all this?" she held it up, questioning.

"I might have enemies." He slid his arms around her waist, still on his knees. He had given her his death in one hand, his life in the other.

"Can I ask?" she whispered.

"You can ask me anything."

"I love you, Jack."

He said nothing.

"Let's go to bed," she said finally, moving to stand. She reached the hallway and turned on the lamp to lead him upstairs. It took a moment for him to adjust to the light, but she reached back and took his hand.